PRAISE FOR *JOSEPH*

NAACP Image Award Nominee

"Will leave readers profoundly moved."
— *Kirkus Reviews*

"Hard-hitting and heartbreaking."
— *BCCB*

"Accessible to . . . reluctant teen readers . . ."
— *School Library Journal*

"Fascinating to read."
— *VOYA*

"The harsh, realistic d   breaking. . . ."
— *Booklist*

". . . [T]he story an
because of his strength and cari
— *Library Media Connection*

JOSEPH

JOSEPH

SHELIA P. MOSES

Margaret K. McElderry Books

New York   London   Toronto   Sydney

MARGARET K. McELDERRY BOOKS

An imprint of Simon & Schuster Children's Publishing Division

1230 Avenue of the Americas, New York, New York 10020

This book is a work of fiction. Any references to historical events, real people, or real locales are used fictitiously. Other names, characters, places, and incidents are products of the author's imagination, and any resemblance to actual events or locales or persons, living or dead, is entirely coincidental.

Copyright © 2008 by Shelia P. Moses

All rights reserved, including the right of reproduction in whole or in part in any form.

MARGARET K. McELDERRY BOOKS is a trademark of Simon & Schuster, Inc.

For information about special discounts for bulk purchases, please contact Simon & Schuster Special Sales at 1-866-506-1949 or business@simonandschuster.com.

The Simon & Schuster Speakers Bureau can bring authors to your live event. For more information or to book an event, contact the Simon & Schuster Speakers Bureau at 1-866-248-3049 or visit our website at www.simonspeakers.com.

Also available in a hardcover edition.

Book design by Cara E. Petrus and Michael McCartney

The text for this book is set in Adobe Garamond.

Manufactured in the United States of America

First paperback edition March 2010

10 9 8 7 6 5 4 3 2 1

The Library of Congress has cataloged the hardcover edition as follows:

Moses, Shelia P.

Joseph / Shelia P. Moses.—1st ed.

p.   cm.

Summary: Fifteen-year-old Joseph tries to avoid trouble and keep in touch with his father, who is serving in Iraq, as he and his alcoholic, drug-addicted mother move from one homeless shelter to another.

ISBN 978-1-4169-1752-6 (hc)

[1. Family problems—Fiction. 2. Mothers—Fiction. 3. Homeless persons—Fiction. 4. Alcoholism—Fiction. 5. Drug abuse—Fiction. 6. African Americans—Fiction.] I. Title.

PZ7.M8475Jo 2008

[Fic]—dc22

2007046464

ISBN 978-1-4169-9442-8 (pbk)

ISBN 978-1-4169-8624-9 (eBook)

R0432157277

To Eric and Emma

CHAPTER ONE

I did not want my new homeroom teacher, Ms. Adams, to shake Momma's hand.

The last time I changed schools, my teacher Mr. Colgate tried to shake my momma Betty's hand, but he noticed the burns on the tips of her fingers. Burns from smoking cigarettes down to the filter. Burns from smoking marijuana every night before she goes to bed. I know Mr. Colgate saw her burns, because he looked at her and frowned. People are always frowning at Momma, and that makes me sad.

Sad that she cannot see herself. Sad that she finds fault in everyone's life except her own.

I wonder how long it will take the people at this school to realize that Momma is a crackhead. I wonder how long it will take them to realize that I feel more like her father than she acts like my momma. When will they realize that we are homeless?

Two days after Mr. Colgate saw Momma's burns, a social worker was standing at the door of our run-down townhouse. The house that stopped being home when Momma ran Daddy away. The social worker said that she had received a call from someone saying that I was living alone and in need of help. That was a lie. They were coming to investigate Momma. Again!

The social worker was coming to see if it was true that I could not let Momma stay alone too long because she cannot take care of herself. Social

Services wanted to see if we had food in the house.

I was really sad that they were treating us like two-year-olds. It did not bother Momma at all that the social worker had stopped by again. She yelled at her and said the same old thing when she left: "What they stopping by here for? I got it going on."

I just looked at her and went to bed. I was ashamed to go to school the next day.

I liked going to Lincoln High School, the school I attended last year for two semesters. But I had to transfer, just like I had to transfer from all the other schools. We never stay in one place too long, not since Daddy left and Granddaddy died.

My new school, Dulles High, is bigger than Lincoln. The counselor says that there are only twenty students in each class and they have a zero tolerance policy here. At Lincoln we had at least thirty-five kids in all of my classes and the students pretty much ran the school. So I know I will like it here. It looks like the teachers are in charge for a change.

The main reason I like it here is no one knows me and they don't know Momma. They do not know that we are living in a homeless shelter. We have been living at the shelter for almost two weeks now.

The people here at Dulles High do not know that Daddy moved to Raleigh before he was deployed to Iraq so that he could get away from Momma. He moved because he could not take it anymore. He could not take the verbal and physical abuse. And he was afraid he would go to jail after Momma was stopped for speeding and the cops found drugs in the car. Of course the car was registered in Daddy's name. I was home watching football with Daddy that Sunday when Five-O knocked on the door. Officer Poole has known Daddy for years, so he had put Momma in the police car and driven her home.

He told Daddy that he had to impound the car and the next time it happened Momma was going back to jail. I wanted to turn the TV off and yell, "There are more drugs in the cookie jar!"

If I had, Momma would not have been stopped by Five-O again two weeks later for a DUI. That time Momma spent sixty days in jail. I felt so sad and alone when she was away. I do not think going to jail bothers her at all. It gives her a chance to see all her friends who are in and out of the county jail for buying and selling dope just like Momma. Daddy knew he would be the next person to go to jail if he stayed with us.

After that Daddy filed for divorce and started fighting for custody of his only child. Me!

The people at this school do not know that my mother is in rehab more than she is at home. She's been in eight times that I am old enough to remember. If she can stay clean this time we can move out of the homeless shelter into our own apartment one day. Maybe I can stay at Dulles High and play tennis. I saw a notice on the board outside of the principal's office about tryouts next week. I'm not great at tennis, but Daddy is, and he taught me a lot on the courts near his house in Raleigh. I have played since I was little, and I want to be a tennis champion one day just like Arthur Ashe. Daddy went to college with Mr. Ashe. Daddy said if I try hard enough, I will be great like Mr. Ashe one day. Of course I plan to get my college degree and my master's, but Momma does not want to hear anything about tennis. She says I should just forget tennis because she thinks I am a better basketball player and I can get rich and buy her a house when I make it to the pros. Her sister, Shirley, told her to never say that to me again.

Aunt Shirley is a lawyer for the city of Durham, and she told Momma that "grades come first" before any sport, including tennis. Aunt Shirley is happy that I want to be a professional tennis player as long as I go to college, too. She tried to take me from Momma several times, just like Daddy did before he got the call from the army that took him halfway across the world.

But Momma told Aunt Shirley that she would never let me live with her. Momma thinks that Aunt Shirley is too uppity. But she is not; she just wants a better life for Momma and me. Aunt Shirley refuses to live in the ghetto and smoke until her teeth are green.

If Daddy were here he would still be fighting for me, because Momma would never willingly give me to him. I found out the real reason Momma wants me to live with her the last time Momma and Aunt Shirley got into an argument.

"My nephew is nothing but a welfare check to you, Betty. You just keep him so you can get child support from Peter and keep using fake names and addresses to get checks and food stamps."

"Get out of my house, Shirley," Momma screamed.

That's when Aunt Shirley said the words that made Momma stop speaking to her for three months.

"I'll go. But before I go, I am calling the Department of Social Services to report you. I should have reported you years ago. Even if you are my sister, I should have reported you when you hit Joseph in the face with that perfume bottle when he was only four years old because he would not stop crying. I should have reported you the first time you used a fake name to get a welfare check."

I stood behind the bathroom door and listened

to Aunt Shirley tell Momma about all the illegal things she has done over the years. I wanted to run out and make her stop talking bad to Momma, but I did not. I knew that it was all true.

I cannot remember all the bad words that Momma said to my aunt after that. I do remember Aunt Shirley crying and saying to Momma, "You are always talking about what Joseph will do for you one day. Why should he buy you a house when you spend your money on drugs and cigarettes?"

Aunt Shirley was saying everything that she ever wanted to say to Momma that day. Things I wanted to say, but wouldn't. Not to my momma.

"And you are going to jail because you lied and told social services that Peter is dead."

How could Momma tell people Daddy is dead? I found out later that she is so desperate that she told several service agencies that Daddy was dead to get on welfare using her maiden name. Momma has no shame. She knows good and well that Daddy is alive and was living in Raleigh until he went overseas. I love Momma, but I do not understand her. I do not understand how she thinks she has it going on. Why does she think I can take care of us? I am only fifteen years old.

I just want a normal life like my cousin Jasmine. She is Aunt Shirley and Uncle Todd's only child. But nothing is normal about my life with Momma. While she is thinking how she has it going on, we are moving, hiding from bill collectors, and stealing food from the corner grocery store. I do not want to live like this for the rest of my life. I want to finish high school and be what Granddaddy called a productive member of society. His name was Joseph too, Joseph P. Peele, and he was a preacher. Momma, Granddaddy, and I were living together until he died.

I miss Granddaddy Joseph. Nothing has been the same since he died and left me at Momma's mercy.

Granddaddy loved sharing his nice house on Simons Street, just two blocks from North Carolina Central University, with us. He said if we lived with him, he could keep an eye on me. Granddaddy said that one day I would go to college at North Carolina Central, just like he did. Just like his brothers did. Just like Aunt Shirley and Jasmine, who is graduating with honors in May.

Momma graduated from North Carolina Central too, but our lives are such that you would think she is a middle-school dropout. She had a job at the IRS for about a year after she graduated, but that did not last long. She was fired from the IRS because they accused her of stealing social security numbers and selling them to her friends, who used them to get credit cards. The IRS could never prove that

Momma did this, but they had enough evidence to fire her. Just not enough to send her to prison. Since then she has changed jobs every year. Of course, it is always someone else's fault. Aunt Shirley told her that day when they were arguing why she could not keep a job, "You run your mouth too much, and no one wants to smell your cigarette breath all day when you are in their face."

Momma does not want to work. Work interferes with her ability to go to happy hour. Happy hour was and still is her favorite time of day. She has been leaving me alone since I was six years old to go out with her friends. Granddaddy and Aunt Shirley stayed on Momma about going back to school to maybe get her master's.

Granddaddy Joseph told Momma that a good education would save her one day. But she did not want to hear that or anything he had to say. She did not like living with Granddaddy as much as I did. She thought he was too bossy, and she wanted to be her own woman. But she cannot be her own woman. He told her that being your own woman means keeping your lights connected for two months straight. Being your own woman means being able to pay your own rent if Peter's check is one day late from Iraq.

The week before we moved in with Granddaddy, we were living in the dark until Aunt Shirley e-mailed Daddy and told him that we did not have lights. He called the power company and had the lights turned back on. Of course Momma was trying to get him to wire her the cash, but he knew better. He would never put money in Momma's hand to pay a bill unless he had to. He just used his credit card to turn the lights on by telephone. He knew Momma would take that money and buy weed or get herself a new dress for happy hour.

"Girl," Granddaddy said with tears in his eyes, "if you want to be your own woman, you got to pray to God to help you. You got to get a job and make something of yourself. Stop using people."

But using people is Momma's only way of survival. She called every friend that Daddy had when he first went to Iraq. She was begging them for money until everyone started telling Daddy and he called her and let her have it. She did not care what Daddy said. She stopped calling Daddy's friends, but when she would run into his friends she'd cry broke until they gave her some money. She did not stop until she ran into Daddy's best friend, Mark, and he did not speak to her. She finally realized that everyone was just tired of her. She called that man a "fat pig" and every curse name in the book.

Granddaddy Joseph and Aunt Shirley were all we had left after Daddy was deployed and Daddy's friends turned their back on Momma. Daddy's family lives in Scotland Neck, North Carolina. They do not want to be bothered with Momma at all. They send me clothes and boxes of food every now and then, but they do not want to talk to Momma again in life. Of course, no one can convince her of that. Every time they have a family event she is trying to catch a ride to Scotland Neck to attend their functions. Functions that it is obvious she is not welcome at. She should focus on her own family, because Daddy's family thinks she is a crackhead just like people at Lincoln High used to say. Granddaddy would tell Momma how much he and her mother, Grandma Millie, loved her. He tried to tell her that she did not need Daddy's family. I have never felt that she needed them at all. She just likes to go around them now to try to get on Daddy's girlfriend Pauline's nerves. Pauline totally ignores Momma and looks at her with pity, if she looks at her at all. Momma needs to just go on with her life.

Granddaddy was always telling Momma to come to his house on the holidays and leave Daddy's family alone. He wanted her to know how much her own family loved her. He said that Grandma really loved Momma. Grandma Millie died from breast cancer before I was born. But Granddaddy kept her pictures all over the house. She was a pretty woman like Momma, but she had grace and style like Aunt Shirley. Her teeth shone like snow in the sunshine. Momma's teeth are stained from the cigarettes and marijuana that she smokes every day.

Granddaddy never understood why Momma kept making the same mistakes over and over again. It was her mistakes that made Daddy leave. I know that Daddy tried to get along with Momma. Besides, he only married her because she was pregnant with me. He knew she was not capable of taking care of a baby, so they got married. Daddy told her he wanted her to get a job so that she would have something to do with her time. He wanted her to stop smoking. He said she needed to stop using the grocery money to buy weed and beer. But Momma is addicted to everything bad and she cannot stop.

Daddy tried hard, and he put Momma in rehab eight times before he gave up. I think he got tired of going to the treatment centers all over North Carolina to visit her. Most of all, he got tired of taking me to see her. Daddy said those centers were no place for a child. I never said this to Momma, but I hated going to those centers more than Daddy hated taking me. I will never forget the day we went to one and Momma was talking out of her head to one of the guards. When she saw us coming she just got louder and pulled up her top and told the guard nasty things. That was the end for Daddy. He turned around and walked away, dragging me along with him.

When Momma got out of the rehab center that time Daddy told her that he was leaving and taking me with him. Momma called the cops and before we could get to the door, cops were everywhere. Poor Daddy stayed because he did not want to leave me behind. He finally gave up after her last arrest, but he never stopped loving me and he did not stop taking care of me. When he gave up and went to Raleigh, he left money in the bank for us to survive, although he paid all the bills. Daddy continued to pick me up every weekend and fought hard to get sole custody. He said he knew the money was too much to give to Momma because of her addictions, but it was enough for emergencies if he was called away to the war. Three months later he was called to duty. Before Daddy even got on the plane, the money he gave Momma was gone.

After Daddy found out that Momma had spent all the money, he still tried to keep up with the bills, but no matter what he did, it was never enough. If he sent money for groceries, Momma was smoking it within an hour. If he sent the money to Aunt Shirley and told her to bring us groceries, Momma would give half of the food to her so-called friend, Aunt Clarine, who is in even worse shape than Momma. She used to be married to Daddy's brother Uncle Ed and they have a son, Ed Jr., who is eighteen years old now. Momma and Clarine like each other because they can sit around and share baby mama drama stories about their husbands who could care less about them. I do not know who made up that term "baby mama drama," but I think they were talking about Momma and Aunt Clarine when they made it up. They are definitely not good mothers and their lives are filled with drama. Both of them will do anything to try to hurt their husbands, who finally had enough of them and their mess. At least Ed Jr. was never hungry, because Uncle Ed took Aunt Clarine to court and proved that she was an unfit mother. Then he moved them both to Alaska to make sure she did not see Ed Jr. too often. Daddy was getting ready to take Momma to court for the third time to fight for custody of me when he was called to Iraq. He missed two court dates because of the stupid war.

I think Daddy felt so helpless after he had to stop living with Momma and me.

After a while Daddy just stopped sending us money and sent it directly to Granddaddy Joseph. Daddy knew Granddaddy would do right by us. When the checks went to Granddaddy's, we did too. Momma found out that Daddy was mailing the checks to Granddaddy's and we moved in with him the next week. Daddy planned it that way. He knows Momma well. He knew that Granddaddy would always take care of me and tell him Momma's every move. The checks came like clockwork from Daddy. He always sent me a letter with the money. I still have most of the letters in my old blue suitcase that Daddy left at the house when he moved to Raleigh.

My dear son Joseph,

How are you? Daddy is doing fine. This war is hard on me, and it is harder to be away from you. I miss seeing you and knowing that I am a short drive away. There is nothing like seeing your face.

I asked your momma about your coming to live with me when I come home and she said no for the hundredth time.

I feel that you need me and I will always need

you. I need to go to work knowing that you had breakfast, and I need to go to sleep knowing that you had a great dinner.

I know that Granddaddy Joseph is doing the best he can, but he is old and should not have to raise my son. I want to raise you. I want to love you and show you how to be a man.

Son, it does not look like this war will end anytime soon. I watch CNN every day trying to keep up with what is going on back home, but it is not the same as being there. I just continue to fight to stay alive, so that I can come home to you.

Love,

Daddy

Three days after I got that letter, Granddaddy was dead. Granddaddy was dead from a heart attack. He died in the place he loved most, First Branches

Baptist Church, over on Monroe Street. Momma had a hangover so she had not gone to church with us that day. I was there when Granddaddy looked out at the congregation from the pulpit and started to sing his favorite song, "Amazing Grace." But nothing came out of his mouth.

I was in the fourth row and saw him grab his chest and fall to the floor. He never woke up. I rode in the ambulance with Granddaddy Joseph and Deacon Willie, but Granddaddy did not know that we were there. The doctors said he was dead when he hit the floor.

Aunt Shirley and Jasmine had not gone to church that Sunday because they had just got back in town from New York, but they met me at the hospital as soon as I called them.

Momma came later with her new boyfriend at the time, Troy, who she had met at Target. She was hollering and crying all over the hospital like a crazy person. I was the only person there who knew she had been cursing at poor Granddaddy all week. She broke his heart. I was happy that Granddaddy did not see her with Troy, because he had been very tired of her moving around and changing men so much.

Momma could care less about Troy. She had just hooked up with him so he would pay the bills that Daddy's child-support checks didn't cover. Every time Troy went to work at Target, Momma called Daddy to bug him for more money and ask him to take her back. She would leave Daddy messages to call her about me. Poor Momma would show Troy how many times Daddy had called her cell phone, trying to make Troy jealous. The truth is, I think that if she were not my mother Daddy would never call Momma again in life.

To make matters worse, Momma found out about Pauline. She is a great artist with a nice art gallery downtown. She is as pretty as the pictures that she paints. So beautiful that she takes my breath away. Of course, I could never say that around Momma. I have to pretend I do not like Pauline to keep Momma happy. Truth is, she is a nice lady. She tried to stay in touch with me after Daddy went to Iraq, but she got tired of Momma's drama and stopped calling.

Just before Daddy left, I took some pictures of me, Pauline, and Daddy in the mountains. I made the mistake of taking them home, and Momma found them. The next thing I knew she had cut them up and mailed them to Pauline's Art Gallery. After that happened, Pauline knew for sure that Momma was crazy. Daddy and Pauline are getting married when he comes home, and I am glad. I love Momma, but I pray every night that she will get off drugs and be a real woman like Pauline. When she is talking junk about Pauline I want to scream, "Shut up, Momma! Don't you see her teeth are not green? Don't you see she cares about me and she is not homeless? Don't you see she is home with her family on the holidays, not begging other people to invite her to their house? Just shut up!"

Even Granddaddy liked Pauline. Granddaddy liked Daddy, too, and said he was a good man and a good father. They talked together a lot before Daddy was deployed. Daddy knows that Granddaddy is dead, but he thinks that Momma and I are still living in Granddaddy's house. Daddy has no idea that we are living in a shelter, but I guess he will find out when he calls Granddaddy's house and the phone is disconnected. For a few months Momma had the calls forwarded to her cell phone because she was never at home, but now the cell phone and the line at Granddaddy's are disconnected. Daddy will call Aunt Shirley when he cannot reach me and she will come to help us. Momma does not have a dime left from her illegal welfare check, and Daddy's check will not come until the first of the month—two weeks from now. I am scared to call my aunt myself because she is sure to call the Department of Social Services.

I wish Momma would help herself before they take me away from her. I cannot let that happen, because she has no one else. Who will take care of her? What if she is not better before I graduate from high school? If she is not better, I guess I am supposed to skip college and get a job taking care of her and sorry Aunt Clarine. I guess that's what Momma thinks, anyway.

If only she had saved the money Granddaddy left us in his will. Granddaddy did not have much money, because he gave most of it to the church. But he left Momma twenty thousand dollars and his house. All she had to do was pay the house note of $340 a month out of the money he left her, and the house would have been paid for in two years.

Granddaddy worked all his life to buy a home for us, and Momma lost it over a few thousand dollars. She never paid one house note and we had to move. At least we moved in August and I didn't have to change schools in the middle of the school year like I've had to before.

Aunt Shirley and Momma had just started speaking again when Aunt Shirley came by and saw the foreclosure sign in the yard at Granddaddy's. Aunt Shirley said she would catch up the payments until she realized that the note was six months behind, plus taxes and insurance. Then she offered to buy the house from Momma, but Momma wanted her sister to pay the six months in mortgage and keep the house in Momma's name. Aunt Shirley refused, and we were evicted while Aunt Shirley was away at a lawyers' conference. Now Aunt Shirley is trying to buy the house back from the bank.

Momma is so comfortable here in this shelter in what she calls the community. She sits around with people who live in this ghetto too, and she brags about being back in the community. I just want to scream. This is not "the community." This is the ghetto. One day she was talking to Clarine on the phone about their "community" and I could not take it anymore. "Momma, stop it!" I said as she lit up another cigarette and started calling Pauline names because she saw an article in the newspaper about her opening a second art gallery. I do not know what came over me, but I grabbed the telephone out of her hand and started screaming.

"Just look out the window at that drug dealer pushing dope to that twelve-year-old boy."

Momma slapped me so hard that I dropped the phone.

"Boy, do not touch this phone again." I do not know what hurt the most, the slap or watching her make a fool out of herself.

She did not talk to me for two days and I was okay with that. I just wanted her to wake up.

Doesn't Momma see what I see when she looks out the window of the shelter? This place is all run-down and the streets are filled with drug addicts and their dealers, people who Momma calls her friends.

I wonder if she knows that I am afraid to walk to the store to get a loaf of bread and that I sleep with a knife under my pillow in case someone breaks into the room we call home.

In our room are a mattress and a hot plate that

we managed to grab before the mortgage company put padlocks on Granddaddy's front door.

The only good thing about being at this shelter is that I am in a school district that buses some of the students to Dulles High, which is two blocks from Duke University here in Durham. It's in an area of town protected from all the things I have to face every day in my neighborhood. The teachers at Dulles High seem serious about education. I think that most teachers at Lincoln were great, but they were afraid of the students, who were basically running the school. Dulles High has none of that. Maybe they can protect me from Momma's mess. This school is too far away from the shelter for her to come over here and yell at these folks and embarrass me like she always does. I just pray that Momma does not mess this up for me.

•   •   •

"Good morning, Ms. Flood. I have been waiting to meet you and Joseph. We are delighted to have him here," Ms. Adams says.

"Oh, you can call me Betty. I ain't old enough for anybody to call me Ms. Flood."

Ms. Adams barely acknowledges Momma making a fool of herself. She just looks at me and smiles.

"Welcome to our campus, Joseph. I understand that you are a good student and that you like tennis."

Before I can answer, Momma is acting the fool.

"Tennis! Who told you that? Don't be talking to him about no tennis. My boy is going to play basketball and go to the pros. I can see him now, girl, and I am going to be Gucci down."

Ms. Adams looks at Momma like she is a man from Mars. Her face says, *Oh, now I know what the problem is.* She smiles a fake smile and says, "Joseph, go inside and take one of the empty seats." Then she turns back to Momma.

"Well, there are many professional tennis players. Besides, with his good grades he can do anything he wants to do and be whatever he wants to be. He does not have to play sports."

"Oh, hell na'll, he in the wrong classroom. You trying to turn him against basketball."

I hang my head and walk away in total shame.

"See you later, dude," Momma yells down the hall as Ms. Adams tells me again to go into the classroom and find a seat.

I know she does not say much to Momma after that, because within minutes Ms. Adams is back in her classroom. I guess she just left Momma standing in the hallway acting like a fool the way most people do when they are tired of her mouth.

I wish Momma had a job to go to. That way she would never come over here.

Every school that I attend becomes Momma's life until people see her for who she really is and then no one wants her around. She has not had a full-time job in years, so she is at every basketball game and every tennis match when she is not high.

I was fine with her being involved at Lincoln High until she agreed to collect the money for T-shirts for the basketball players. She did collect the money, and just like always she messed things up.

During the first game, Mr. Faison saw Daddy and approached him on the basketball bleachers.

"Sir, your wife collected thirty dollars from me and twenty other parents weeks ago for T-shirts for our players. The parents decided we did not want T-shirts after all, and we wanted the money back to buy snacks to sell at the games instead, but no one has been reimbursed by Betty. We have asked her several times to give us the money back."

Daddy was so embarrassed. I was injured that night and was sitting with Daddy before the game started as he made it clear to Mr. Faison that Momma was no longer his wife. Then he paid him the money that Momma owed him. Pauline was there too. She did not say anything. She just looked embarrassed for me.

The kids teased me for the rest of that week about my mother taking the T-shirt money and laughed at Momma when they saw her. I was so hurt that she would steal from my classmates' parents. I was embarrassed to even go to school the next day. I just kept my head down until the kids found something new to talk about.

The most hurtful part was that it did not bother Momma at all that she had embarrassed me.

CHAPTER TWO

"Class, we have a new student. His name is Joseph Flood, and I want you all to welcome him at lunchtime," Ms. Adams says.

The kids smile at me and I smile back. But I know that some of them will stop smiling when they find out that the clothes on my back are the only clothes that I have. My other clothes are locked in Granddaddy's house that has a foreclosure sign in the yard. Somehow they will find out that we are in the homeless shelter, and they will laugh at us. I look at my new classmates and wonder how long it will take for them to learn the truth.

I look at the pretty girl sitting to my left. She has her name, Melanie, written on her gym bag.

Melanie says hi when I first sit down. She looks so nice and clean. She will never talk to someone who lives in a homeless shelter like me. I have to get out of that shelter before someone finds out the truth.

Maybe I should e-mail Daddy, if I can use the computer in the library today. If I do that, he will surely call DSS and they will take me away from Momma. As much as I want to get away from her and that one room in the shelter, I do not want her to be alone. If she is alone, there will be no one to put out her burning cigarette at night so that she does not burn herself to death. Who will make sure that she does not drink too much? Who will love Momma?

Lunchtime is different here at Dulles High. The students are not running around like they are crazy, and the food looks pretty good.

Last week, Ms. Monet, who used to be Momma's best friend in high school, told me that this is a good high school when she heard I had transferred here. I ran into her and her daughter at Wal-Mart. Valerie is a senior at Dulles and she is really cute like Melanie.

Ms. Monet is a nice lady, but she looked at me real strange when she saw me checking out that cute daughter of hers and I know why. My home life isn't good enough for Valerie. Ms. Monet has never said it to me; it was in her eyes. Her eyes were saying, *You are a nice boy, but your mother is a crackhead. . . . You are a nice boy, but you live in a shelter. . . . You are a nice boy, but your mother smokes a pack of cigarettes a day. . . . She has baby mama drama and no one wants to be bothered with her.*

Then she looked at me and she was reminded of what is good.

"How is school? Do you like being a sophomore? Have you heard from your daddy? How's your Aunt Shirley?"

Momma saw us talking and came running over to put her two cents in.

"Girl, his daddy ain't no good, what you asking about him for?" That same old mess.

Ms. Monet looked at Momma and walked away.

Momma is always mad at Ms. Monet because Ms. Monet told her to stop bugging Daddy with her mess. Ms. Monet is fine when Momma is not speaking to her. That way Ms. Monet does not have to worry about Momma borrowing money from her again in life.

Ms. Monet has been divorced from Valerie's daddy for years. Valerie told me that they are not friends, but her parents are friendly. Ms. Monet does not bug Valerie's daddy like Momma bugs Daddy. When Daddy was living in Raleigh, Momma called him all day, every day. She did it just to get on his nerves. She wanted to talk about everything with him except me.

"Did you send the check?"

"Where were you?"

"I bet you went out of town with Pauline."

Momma even goes on the Internet at the library to see what Pauline is doing at her art galleries.

I know now that Momma is the true essence of what the kids at school call "Baby Mama Drama" and she does not even know it.

When I was young I did not understand, and I always thought my daddy was the bad guy. But the older I get, the more I realize that Momma hates Daddy because he does not want her. The older I get, the more I understand that he only married her because she was pregnant. If I know that, Momma knows that. One thing they both have taught me is to never have kids until after you walk down the aisle.

Even though I know all of this, I hate to watch Momma begging for his time. She is pitiful the way she calls him like he is the only man in the world. I always know when Momma is calling him when I am with him. Daddy looks at the caller ID and does not answer. When Pauline calls, he smiles and says, "Hey, baby," when he picks up the phone. Poor Momma is always talking about Daddy ain't thinking about Pauline, but I do not hear him calling Momma "baby."

She should think about that one.

Momma should just take her child support checks and let Daddy go. She needs a new start and so do I. I hope my new start is here at Dulles High.

Even the chairs in the cafeteria are nicer than in my old school.

"Hi, Joseph, I'm Nick," the guy sitting next to me says, "and this is my best friend, Paul."

Nick is white and Paul is black. You would never see this at my old school. Everything there was divided by the color of your skin. Granddaddy Joseph always said that God did not want us to be apart like that.

"Nice to meet you both," I say as I bite down on my cheeseburger and reach for my wedge potatoes. I am so hungry. Nick has two burgers. I should have asked for two. We could never have this much food at my old school, and we definitely could not ask for seconds.

"Do you play football?" Nick asks.

"No, man, I shoot a little basketball, but tennis is my thing." White guys always think that brothers can only play basketball and football, but I have played tennis since I was about four years old. I think I love it so much because Daddy gave me a tennis racquet, and he would take me to the courts with him every weekend.

"Cool, man," Nick says. "I'm on the tennis team. We're pretty good. Tryouts are next week. You should give it a try. Now, my boy Paul here could care less about sports—he is Mr. Academic. Straight A's since elementary school."

Maybe I was wrong about the white guys thinking that brothers can only play basketball and baseball.

"Straight A's, that's pretty cool," I say. "If I could get that math down, I could have straight A's. Last semester at my old school I had all A's and one B."

Paul finally says something. "Hey, man, I'll tutor you sometime if you want me to."

"That would be cool," I answer as we finish our lunch.

If they only knew how hard it is to keep my grades up trying to survive the streets with Momma. I am not accustomed to guys wanting to tutor each other. At Lincoln High that was just a way for the guys and girls to get together to hang out. The guys were always trying to tutor girls that they wanted to date.

The day goes by fast as the students walk down the nice hallway like they don't have a worry in the world. They all look full, like lunch was not their first meal of the day. Just before last period I run into Nick again on his way to English class. "Joseph, the list to sign up for tennis is in the gym," he says. "You should put your name on it."

"Thanks for the info, man. I will sign up tomorrow." I'm excited about trying out for that team.

When the last bell rings, I walk outside and wait for bus number 95. That's the bus that will take me and sixteen other students who do not belong on this side of town back twenty miles to our neighborhoods. For me, it's back to the shelter to suffer until morning.

The bus stops at the corner grocery store near the shelter and I get off so that the other kids will not see me walk into the shelter. Their lives are bad too, but at least they have a home. Well, I pray that they do.

A few other kids are coming into the shelter after school too, but I must be the only high school student here, because I do not see anyone that I know from my first day at Dulles High. I stop at the front desk and sign back in for the evening and walk down the long hallway that leads to the stairway. The steps are dirty and no one seems to even notice me as I walk in between the men who are sitting on the steps, eating.

"Hey, Momma," I say as I walk into our room.

Putting out the smoldering cigarette in the ashtray next to the mattress on the floor, I touch Momma on the back when she does not answer. I do not know how she sleeps like that. She sleeps all day and she is up all night. I guess she is bored now because all the phones are off. Before, she could sit on the phone and talk about nothing all day with Clarine, trying to figure out what their ex-husbands were doing with their new girlfriends. They say really bad things about my daddy's family. Funny thing is, Daddy's family all have jobs, they go to church, and their children are not hungry. Daddy's family has just washed their hands of Momma and crazy Clarine.

"Hey, dude, did you have a good day?" Momma asks as she rolls over on the mattress, still wearing the clothes she had on when she went with me to school this morning. I hate it when she calls me dude; like we are friends, instead of mother and son.

"I had a good day, Momma. This school is really cool and they have a tennis team. "

She doesn't even look at me. She never does. When she gets mad she is always saying, "You look just like your crazy daddy." I think she cannot stand the sight of me most of the time because I do look like Daddy.

"Momma, the lunch is really good at Dulles."

"Well, that's good, because there ain't no food in this room. That lunch will have to last until tomorrow morning, unless you want to eat that nasty mess they serve in the kitchen."

I rub the oatmeal cookie in my pocket that I saved from lunch. My dinner.

CHAPTER THREE

The next morning I get up early to go through the box of used clothes in the hallway at the shelter. I find an old polo shirt to wear with the jeans that I wore yesterday.

I think about Daddy as I stand in line waiting to use the iron and ironing board. I wonder if he has tried to call our old number. I know that he is worried by now.

Man, I am so hungry. I know if I arrive at school early I can eat a good breakfast. I missed breakfast yesterday because Momma and I were talking to Ms. Adams, but not today. I do not know what it is like to get a good meal in the morning unless I am with Daddy or Aunt Shirley. They both cook me a full meal, and I drink all the orange juice that my stomach can hold at their houses.

I am standing at the corner waiting when the bus arrives. I cannot let the kids from Dulles High see me leaving the shelter. Maybe they will think I live in the white house with the fence that is right beside the shelter. Even in the hood the families that live here try to make their houses look good.

"Joseph Flood," Ms. Adams says like she is happy to be at school.

"Present," I answer.

She smiles at me and calls the next student's name.

This is different from my old schools too. They

never even bothered to call the roll at Lincoln. The principal said if you were too lazy to come to class, his teachers were too busy to waste time on roll call. I told Granddaddy what the principal said. He did not like that too hot, but he thought about it a minute and said, "Grandson, I do not know this man, but he is telling you that people who are serious about their life are always in place and always on time. You forget about that roll call and just show up. Show up on time. Half the battle, boy, is just showing up."

I remember things like that, things my Granddaddy tried to teach me. Things that keep me from feeling like a loser. Granddaddy was always praising my daddy for being such a good man and a good soldier. Granddaddy said that it is very important not to wait for people to take care of you. "Do not wait on the mountain to come to you—climb the mountain yourself." Granddaddy said that every day of his life. Momma is always waiting on the mountain and mad at people who are climbing their own mountain. Maybe she should stop being mad and climb the mountain too.

After our English class, Paul and Nick wait for me in the hallway. The classes here are much easier than at Lincoln. The teachers are able to focus on the students without having to tell them to be quiet for a full hour.

"Hey, man, we are going to math class. What's next for you?" Nick asks.

"Math," I say.

"You want to walk with us?"

"Sure," I say, and they both give me a high five.

We get to class early and talk about the class before the teacher comes in.

"Man, Ms. Rowe is strict, but don't worry, I'll help you get that A."

It's cool to be around people who actually want to help each other. I look over at the other students.

The kids here do not spend a lot of money on clothes, but they look nice. Most of the guys wear jeans and polo shirts. The girls wear jeans too, but not the tight ones like the honeys at my old schools. Daddy always reminded me that women who display their bodies so much usually do not have much of a brain. He said that is how his brother, Uncle Ed, got stuck with Clarine. Ed thought Clarine had a nice body when she was young, but she was as dumb as a doorknob. Uncle Ed loves his son, but I know he regrets that Clarine is Ed Jr.'s mother.

The last time I saw Ed Jr. he did not even want to visit his mother anymore. We were at Granddaddy's funeral. I thought it was nice of them to come, since they are really not related to Granddaddy and they live so far away in Alaska.

"Hey, man, your momma is over there standing with my momma. Let's go over and say hi," I suggested.

"Yeah, man, I saw her earlier," Ed said as he moved closer to the funeral director's car so that his momma could not see him.

"Man, that's your momma. I cannot believe you do not want to hang out with her."

Ed just looked at me. Then he said, "Man, you are going to wake up one day just like I did. Our mommas ain't right and they are not good for us."

When I told Daddy what Ed Jr. had said, Daddy said the same thing he said when we had our birds and bees talk. One thing he said that I will always try to remember is, "Boy, don't you sleep with every girl that takes her skirt off for you. If she is fourteen or fifteen, more than likely she has started her monthly cycle. If she has her cycle she can become a mother.

That means you are the daddy. Do not sleep with any girl who you do not want to be the mother of your child ten years from now."

I know Daddy was talking about his own situation. I know he wishes my mother were more like Aunt Shirley. I know that he is embarrassed that he has a child with Momma just like Uncle Ed is embarrassed. He has to be, because as much as I love my momma I am embarrassed by her too. I am not dating anyone right now. What's the use? I do not want to be embarrassed by that, too. Daddy should not worry about me and girls. I do not even have a phone number to give a girl. When I do start dating, I want it to be with a nice girl like Jasmine or Melanie, or maybe someone like Valerie.

I do not want to ever live like this again. I want to live better. I want Momma to live better. Like normal people. I want to make new friends like Paul and Nick. I tried to make friends at Lincoln, but most of the guys there were troublemakers.

I hung out with some of the Lincoln guys a little until Thanksgiving last year, when my neighbor, Matthew, got shot while trying to rob the corner grocery store. I liked Matthew, but he did not like himself. He stayed in trouble and never went to school. When he did come to class, he was always late and never turned in his homework.

Every time Daddy saw Matthew he would say the same thing to me. "Do not hang around that boy. There are two places for Matthew. Jail or the graveyard."

Daddy said he saw trouble all over Matthew's face. Momma told Daddy to shut up and that Matthew was just as good as everyone else. Maybe Momma was right and Matthew was as good as me, but he was trouble and now he is dead. It could have been me.

On the same day that he was shot to death, Matthew had asked me to go with him to that grocery store. I thought about what Daddy said about being in the wrong place at the wrong time, and I stayed on the basketball court down the street from where I was living with Momma at the time. In the ghetto! The neighborhood had gone down from when Daddy lived with us. I heard a gunshot and I knew it was Matthew. I did just what Granddaddy had told me not to do. I ran right into trouble.

When I got to Reid's Grocery Store, Matthew was lying on the sidewalk. He had tried to run with the money bag that he grabbed out of Mr. Reid's hand as Mr. Reid was trying to lock it up in the safe-deposit box under the counter. Matthew had on a ski mask, so Mr. Reid did not know it was a kid from the hood. Mr. Reid was just trying to shoot the bag out of the kid's hand, but Matthew jumped behind a car and the bullet hit the car and ricocheted into his chest.

Everybody in the neighborhood ran to Mr. Reid's store within minutes to see another brother dead on the sidewalk.

Before I could run back home, people started picking up rocks and knocking all of Mr. Reid's windows out of his store.

But Mr. Reid never put his gun down. With tears in his eyes, he kept yelling, "A man's got the right to protect his property!"

Momma hated Mr. Reid after that, but Daddy didn't. He said he was sorry that Matthew was dead, but it was his job to protect me and get me out of that neighborhood. Daddy had been trying to get Momma to move for a long time because the neighborhood had changed since we all lived there together. He said the neighborhood had gone downhill and she did not need to be over there with me living like a dog. But living like a dog suits Momma and Clarine just fine. I think Momma would have lived there forever if Daddy had not stopped sending her checks there.

I went to Matthew's funeral at Granddaddy's church, and every drug dealer in town came. Matthew had hung out with those guys and called them his family. His mother had died years ago from an over-dose and his daddy is serving twenty-five years for armed robbery.

After the funeral, I went back to our neighbor-hood and helped a group of guys paint R.I.P. MATT on the side of a building. Momma looked at it and said, "That's cool, dude."

Daddy came to pick me up the next day and saw the words on the building. He was real mad.

"Joseph, did you have anything to do with those

words been painted on the building?" Daddy asked very angrily when I got in his SUV.

"I helped some guys to do it. We wanted to honor Matthew."

Daddy pulled his SUV back into the parking lot where I lived and looked at me real hard. He was trying not to say the wrong thing.

"Son, I am sorry that your friend is dead. But he died just like he lived, and you have no right to glorify his death by destroying someone else's property."

Momma was hanging out the window when she saw Daddy pull over in the parking lot to talk to me. As usual, she had to find out Daddy's business. She ran down the stairs to Daddy's side of the SUV and asked what was going on. When Daddy told her what happened and that he was giving two months of my allowance to the building manager to pay for the damage, Momma started cussing at him and said,

"Big shot, you need to give that money to me. I need a new car. And any other extra money you have, you need to give that to me too."

My boys Marcus and Raymond were on their way to the basketball court when they got a ringside seat to see Momma acting the fool. They laughed when they saw Momma standing there in the parking lot, cussing Daddy out. Daddy drove off with me in the SUV and left her just standing there. When he brought me home that evening, she was hanging out of the window again with a cigarette in one hand and a phone in the other, talking her baby mama drama. Talking to Clarine, of course. She cussed at Daddy some more from the window. Daddy drove off, and he never mentioned Matthew to me again.

You know Marcus and Raymond went to school and told the other boys what had happened with

Momma. There is no time better than lunchtime to jone on your friends.

"Yo, man, what's up with your moms?" Marcus asked me as Raymond laughed.

"Yeah, man, she went off on your pops. If that was my dad, he would have got out of that car and run my moms all over that parking lot," said Raymond.

"Yo, she is what you call a 'ghetto momma,'" Marcus added.

The next thing I knew we all were in the principal's office and kicked out of school for three days for fighting. I know my momma ain't right and all, but I could not let them talk about her like that.

Daddy was not happy. He told Momma it was her fault for acting like a fool and it was my fault for responding to fools. But Daddy does not know what it is like to have to be a father to your mother. He grew up in a home with my grandma Tilly and grandpa Thomas. They are both dead now, but they were good people and they were always there for Daddy and Ed and their sisters and brothers. Daddy does not know how many friends I have lost because they say bad things about Momma and I fight with them. Maybe I will find some new friends at Dulles and we can stay friends and go to college together. Maybe Nick and Paul really want to be friends.

Momma changes friends just like she changes clothes, except for Clarine. They are two hens in a nest. Momma pretends she is friends with people until she borrows money and does not pay them back. After she cannot pay them back, she starts picking fights with them so that she will never have to give the money back. She owes everybody money except Ms. Monet, because she stopped loaning her money years ago. Granddaddy said that borrowing money from folks is the best way to lose a friend.

"Loan them money and you have lost a friend if they do not pay you back."

The last straw for Ms. Monet was when she bought me a coat for my birthday once and Momma claimed it was too big. She called Ms. Monet on her job to ask for the receipt so that she could take the coat back to the store. Ms. Monet knew that Momma was just trying to get the receipt so she could return the coat and get the money, so Ms. Monet told Momma no.

Ms. Monet saw Granddaddy at the grocery store after that and told him all about the coat and how crazy Momma acted. Granddaddy called Momma and really let her have it that night. Momma responded, "Monet just mad because I look better than she does. She is jealous of me." Granddaddy could not believe he was hearing her say that. He hung up the phone and prayed for two hours.

Granddaddy knew a lot about life, if you just took the time to listen to him. The problem with Momma was very simple to him. Grandma had died when Momma was young, and Momma was not willing to take responsibility for her own life. She needs someone to blame. Anybody—as long as the problem is not her fault.

I am trying not to be that way. Maybe new friends at this new school will be good. Paul and Nick sure are nice.

Nick slips me a note in math class: "There is a dance on Friday night. You should hang out with us."

I write him back, "Yeah, man, but I have tennis tryouts first."

This dance will give me a chance to get to know some of the other students.

After school I catch the bus to my corner store

and walk in the direction of the pretty white house. When the bus is out of sight I start walking toward the shelter, but change my mind and walk all the way to Granddaddy's house so that I can check the mailbox.

A letter from Daddy.

Dear Son,

I do hope that you will go to your granddaddy's house and get this letter out of the mailbox. I have been trying to reach you for two weeks. Your aunt Shirley is at a conference, but she should be back by the time you receive this letter. I talked to her and she said she would find you as soon as she gets back.

It is so hard to be away from you. It is hard knowing that you are not okay. Each day I fight for my life in this war. I fight to come home to you. I am afraid, but I believe God will let me come home. He will let me come home to you.

My friend Al was injured yesterday. That really scared me. They are taking him out of this jungle tonight. Injured or not, at least he can go home to his wife and children.

Are you eating, son? How are your grades? Love you and need to find you.

Love,

Daddy

CHAPTER FOUR

On Friday I do not bother to go back to the shelter after school. I know that Momma will be hanging out with Clarine at happy hour anyway. I go to the gym and change clothes like all the other kids are doing who are trying out for tennis.

Coach Williams is cool. I can tell from the way he is talking to us.

"All right, Joseph, let me see what you got. April is one of the best players we have; let's see if you can beat her."

I cannot believe this. All of these guys out here and he has me playing against a girl. A six-foot-tall girl.

I try to remember my down-the-line drills and keep the pace of hitting the ball at least twenty-five times in a row. April is definitely following the rules. Daddy said you have to play tennis at least twice a week to keep up with this game. That's hard to do when you are living in a shelter.

"Good, good, Joseph, good," Coach keeps screaming from the bench.

When April is finished beating me, the girls cheer and the guys laugh. I do not care because I know I played a good match.

Coach looks at me and smiles.

"Did I make the team, Coach?" I ask.

"Not yet, son. Come back on Monday."

I am excited as I run to take a shower to get ready for the dance.

• • •

Even Dulles dances are different from the dances at Lincoln. The students dress nice and the guys are not walking around in their gang colors. I was always afraid to go to the Lincoln dances after a few bad fights broke out last year. After every dance you had to worry about being caught outside the dance hall and having to defend yourself against a gang member or one of the school bullies.

I am having a good time dancing with Melanie until I spot some guys from Lincoln across the dance floor. Guys I do not want to see. I do a quick move with the Bankhead Bounce and turn my back to the guys from Lincoln as Melanie is doing the Cabbage Patch all over the place. She can really dance, but somebody needs to tell her that the Cabbage Patch went out two years ago.

"Arthur and Anthony," I say as the twins spot

me and start walking across the dance floor. *What are they doing here?* I am thinking. They are the last two people I want to see. They are both trouble-makers, and they are both out of jail on bond. Now these two cats are really too dumb to be criminals. A few months ago they robbed a gas station over on Highland Boulevard. The bad part is they were wearing their Lincoln High football jackets with their numbers on the back. The station manager wrote their numbers down, and they were arrested at school the next day. They got kicked out of Lincoln, so I don't know what they are doing at Dulles.

"Hey, Joseph, man," Arthur and Anthony say at the same time.

"Hey, you guys going to school here now?" I ask as I try to keep dancing with Melanie. I am praying that they will say no.

"Yeah, man, we got kicked out of Lincoln for now. We're using our aunt's address so that we can go to school over here."

They are so crazy, they just start dancing with each other and talking to me. I want to ask them how they got into another public school, but it is not my business and I really do not care. I know better than to get caught up with them. Daddy would not be happy about that. I just Bankhead Bounce as far away from them as possible as they yell and scream like they used to at Lincoln.

"Party over here!" they both yell. They are acting so out of place here at Dulles.

We party until midnight. The girls are pretty here, and they follow the school dress code: pants high and blouse low, no belly buttons in sight. No low-riding jeans at Dulles.

I like hanging out with Melanie, who does not

seem to mind being around me. That is because she does not know the truth.

I hope my clothes look okay. The guys' dress code here is not that bad: A belt every day and no shirt on the outside. I see nothing wrong with wearing a shirt on the outside, but I always had to wear my shirt on the inside around Daddy and Granddaddy, so it's just another day for me.

As soon as the dance is over, I hear a noise outside the gym. I know that sound. Trouble! The sound of a fight. I just know that the twins are involved.

Just like Granddaddy said, you can leave a problem, but it will come and find you. When I get outside and see that the twins are fighting, I cannot believe it. The twins are beating up Paul and Nick! Beating them bad. Beating them for no reason at all. Melanie and all the other girls are screaming and crying and the teachers are trying to break up the fight. Coach Williams is the only one who can pull those crazy twins off of Paul and Nick. As soon as he pulls one twin up, the other one jumps back in swinging.

Paul is trying to hold his own as he swings at them over and over, but Nick is taking a beating.

I try to help by grabbing Anthony's arm.

"Chill out, man," I yell.

He looks at me like a madman.

"Get your hands off of me," he says as he stops knocking on Nick's head and starts knocking on mine.

Saved by the school police. The twins are grabbed within minutes, but so am I, as I feel one of the police officers' hands gripping my arm.

"Hey, why are you grabbing me?" I yell as they put handcuffs on me. "I didn't do anything."

The officer is not looking at me. He is looking at

my Lincoln High jacket; it's just like the ones the twins are wearing. I wear it because it is the only one I have. Melanie tries to defend me, but the police officer will not listen. He just keeps looking at my jacket.

Wrong place, wrong time, I am thinking as they lead us all away from the school to the police cars. They are taking Nick and Paul, too.

The ride to the police station is long.

I have never been arrested before.

I think about Daddy all the way there. I know he will be so disappointed when he finds out about this.

Paul and Nick's parents are at the station before we can even get in the door. But they are not alone. Several students and some teachers have followed them to the station to tell them that Paul and Nick did nothing wrong.

When they read me my rights they say I can make one phone call, but I have no one to call. Daddy is halfway around the world; Momma's cell phone is off. So I have no choice. I have to call Aunt Shirley. I am praying she is back from her conference. The call goes into her voice mail.

I have to fill out this stupid paper with all of my information on it. I do not have an address, so I put down Daddy's full name and old address in Raleigh. When I look up, I see Officer Poole sitting in the break room having coffee.

Officer Poole looks over and spots me.

"What you doing here, Joseph?" he asks as he walks toward me. I tell him what happened. He says he can't bail me out because he is on duty. Then they take me away. I whisper the name of the shelter to Officer Poole, and I know he will find a way to reach Aunt Shirley.

When the twins' momma, Ms. Cane, comes for them, she bails me out too, using her house for bail.

"You need a ride home, son?" Ms. Cane asks as she slaps both twins in the back of their heads with her purse. Ms. Cane is old school, because she uses the purse on me too.

"No, ma'am, I don't need a ride."

I am not about to let her drop me off at the shelter. The twins will tell everyone at Dulles that I am homeless. I thank her for bailing me out, and I promise her that my daddy will call her if I owe her any money. Well, as soon as I can reach Daddy.

I walk all the way back to the shelter.

Every wino in town must be on the street tonight. I turn the corner on Maple Street and see a drug deal going down. My heart stops when a big dude in a Mercedes looks me in the eyes.

"Keep your mouth closed!" he says. He looks like the devil to me.

I keep walking and praying for my life. I am actually glad to see the shelter when I finally make it there. I never thought I would be glad to see this shelter. Tonight I am glad to be here and alive.

For the first time in my life, Momma is home before I am on a Friday night.

"Where you been, dude?" she says as she gets up off the mattress, still wearing her party clothes. "Do you know what time it is?" she asks before I can answer her first question.

"I know it's late, Momma, but I got arrested because I had on this Lincoln jacket and the Cane twins had on the same one and they got in a fight and—"

Momma looks at me. "Why were you out in the streets?"

I can't believe she said that. She is *always* in the streets.

"I went to the school dance, and the twins from Lincoln High started a fight with some guys. I did nothing wrong."

This is when the yelling starts.

She yells and yells, telling me that I am no good just like my Daddy. I tune her out and pray that morning will come sooner.

CHAPTER FIVE

Somehow Officer Poole reaches Aunt Shirley. I knew he would.

I can hear Aunt Shirley talking to the counselor at the shelter early the next morning. I open my door and peek outside. Aunt Shirley is standing at the shelter door with her hands on her hips, mad as all get-out.

"I am here to find my nephew, Joseph Flood."

Momma hears her sister's voice too.

I can barely get out of the doorway in time when Aunt Shirley storms past me.

"Get your stuff, Joseph," she says. She never looks down at Momma, who still has a hangover from last night. But Momma looks up at her sister.

"You do not have a child in this room, Shirley, and if you try to take mine, I will call the police."

That is kind of funny to Aunt Shirley, because she knows that the last thing on earth Momma is going to do is call the police.

They have never been scared of each other. Aunt Shirley promised Momma that she was going to get her one day for all the bad she had done to me. Maybe that day is today.

"Shut up, Betty. I did not come here to talk to you. I came for Joseph."

"You can talk all day, but my child stays here."

"Why does he stay? Because you have given the welfare department this address too. I tell you what, Betty, you give him to me now or I am turning you in to DSS Monday morning."

That gets Momma's attention. She has spent a lifetime on and off of welfare because of all her lies. She knows if the government ever catches her, she is done for. Daddy told Granddaddy that she owed them well over forty-six thousand dollars. Even when they were married and I was much younger, she was using Clarine's fake address to get checks that Daddy did not find out about until last year. She would die if she knew that I overheard Daddy telling Granddaddy about those checks. That rapper, 50 Cent, said, "Parents think children see nothing. We see everything." That is so true.

I want to go with my aunt. But I have seen enough to know that I cannot leave Momma. I just want to go someplace to eat and come back. I am hungry! If Momma had any money for our breakfast she spent it at happy hour last night.

I stand there and listen to them argue until my cousin Jasmine walks in with a bag of food. She had been circling the block trying to find a parking space. Poor thing, she looks horrified. She is not used to this bad neighborhood.

"Hi, cousin," she says as she smiles at me.

"Hey, Jasmine," I say as I try to calm her down.

We hug and walk outside where we listen to the two sisters argue for another thirty minutes. I can hear Aunt Shirley telling Momma that she sent Daddy an e-mail about my address. I eat the breakfast she brought me from Waffle House. I have to save Momma some food.

Momma comes to the door and says to me, "As much as I have done for you, I know you would not leave me."

Done for me? I am thinking. She sees things so differently from everyone around her.

"We should both go, Momma."

"They don't want me at their house. They came
for you."

Jasmine is crying now.

"We can't leave Aunt Betty, Momma," she says in
between tears.

"Betty, you can come too, but you have to leave
your drinking, smoking, and getting high at the door."

"Hell, I will never live with you," Momma says
with a laugh and goes back into the shelter.

Aunt Shirley looks at me and says, "Joseph, this
is no way to live. I know you love your mother, but
this is wrong. Take Jasmine's phone—I will get her
a new one—and call me whenever you are ready to
leave this place. And don't take too long. You don't
have to live like this. You can come and live with us.
Your Uncle Todd wants you to come with us."

Her husband is a good guy and I know he would

be okay with me living with them. He has always wanted a son. I want to say, *I thought Daddy was going to call.* But I do not say anything. Aunt Shirley looks at me and whispers, "I will call you on three-way when your daddy calls."

She looks over at Momma, who is standing in the doorway with her hands on her hips, and gives her sister the evil eye. As Aunt Shirley is walking away, her phone rings. It is Daddy, and he asks to speak to me.

I can barely hear him with the overseas connection, but I do hear him say, "Go with your aunt."

"Daddy, I can't leave Momma."

"Son, I am going to lose this connection in a minute. You go like I tell you."

Then I hear the dial tone.

Aunt Shirley looks at me like I should just walk away from Momma. And maybe I should, but not today. I want to spend the night and try to convince her to come with me.

"What are you going to do?" my aunt asks. She is not giving up after she knows Daddy is totally on her side.

"I need to stay here with Momma."

I know that they do not understand, but I have all of them to love me and they are so tired of Momma that she has only me, unless you count Clarine. I have always done what Daddy told me to do, but I cannot leave Momma.

I look at Aunt Shirley again. "She needs me, Auntie."

"That's just *her* need, not your need, boy. She needs to take care of herself and you can come home with me and live a normal teenage life."

Momma is madder now than before. She is mad because Daddy did not ask to speak to her. She is always grabbing the phone when he calls. She is too bitter to realize that the only reason she keeps trying to talk to him is she loves him. She should have been nicer to him and maybe he would have tolerated her until I was grown.

My aunt looks at us both, shakes her head, and walks away with Jasmine following her in tears again. Poor Jasmine would cry herself to death if she was around this mess every day. Aunt Shirley stops on the sidewalk.

"Joseph, I will pick you up for church at ten o'clock tomorrow morning," she says as she tries to comfort Jasmine with a big hug.

"Church! That's funny." Momma's running her mouth.

I say good-bye to them as Momma rolls her eyes and walks back inside again.

Momma does not say a word to me the rest of

the day. She knows that I wanted to go with them. I eat from the other bag of food they left me while Momma calls Clarine on Jasmine's phone.

"Child, now Shirley is acting like she is Peter's sister, not mine."

I can't believe her. You would think Momma does not have a worry in the world. I sure hope Jasmine has free weekend minutes on that cell phone.

CHAPTER SIX

Momma fell asleep talking to Clarine last night.
I am back at Granddaddy's First Branches Baptist
Church for the first time in a long time.

"Hey, Joseph, you're looking like your daddy," Ms.
Nettie says as soon as she spots me coming up the steps.

"Hey, Ms. Nettie. How are you?"

"I am fine, son. It is good to see you. We have
been praying for your daddy." Then she is going
on and on about Daddy and how much they miss
Granddaddy Joseph.

Everyone is glad to see me. Not one person asks about Momma. People are always glad when she is not around to talk loud and make a fool out of both of us. I am glad too, so that I can spend time with people who really like me. I see a lot of Daddy's friends. Over the years I have learned the difference between Momma's hatred for Daddy's family and friends and how they feel about me.

Aunt Shirley and Jasmine are smiling when they see all the people hugging me and welcoming me back to church.

I feel a little out of place because it has been so long since I have been here. Granddaddy might come back from the dead because I am not wearing a suit. I do not have one. I got this white shirt and these black pants out of the shelter's donation box late last night, and this will have to do.

I can still see Granddaddy standing in the pulpit

singing and preaching at the same time. I can still see the women shouting and the men saying, "Yes, sir, preach, preach."

After church I go home with Aunt Shirley for lunch. Of course, I hang around for dinner, too.

"You want some food to take with you, cousin?" Jasmine asks after we eat.

I want to take Momma a plate, so I pretend I am taking two servings for myself. When I start filling the doggie bag with leftovers, Jasmine and Aunt Shirley look at each other and shake their heads. They know I am taking food to Momma. They caught on to me a long time ago and know that I take Momma food from wherever I can get it.

"Here, cousin, take two plates. You might be hungry again before bedtime," Jasmine says with a smile. I sure hope she does not start that crying again. They really love Momma too, but they do not approve of her ghetto lifestyle.

Jasmine does not understand why I have to live this way. It is hard for her to understand because she has always had her parents to take care of her, not the other way around.

All the way back to the shelter I say nothing to my aunt and cousin. It is always silent when they take me back to Momma. When we drive up into the parking lot at the shelter, Momma is sitting in the second-floor window talking on the phone and smoking a cigarette. I do not have to guess who she is talking to. And she is using Jasmine's phone again. I left it at home because I was going to church. That was a mistake.

Aunt Shirley is looking up at the window now. "Where is Jasmine's phone, Joseph?" she asks in a very angry voice. Then she yells, "Never mind!" and jumps out of the car, with Jasmine and me running behind her.

Aunt Shirley races up the stairs into the room, walks in without knocking, and tries to grab the phone out of her sister's hand. Momma is not letting go of that phone.

The arguing starts again until one of the shelter staff members comes in and makes Aunt Shirley and Jasmine leave. Momma never even stops talking to Clarine on that phone.

"You know what, Clarine? My sister is going to make me hurt her. She makes me sick with her uppity self."

Momma did not say "Hello" to me. No "How was church?" Just the same mess with Clarine.

They have to be the two most miserable people in the world.

•   •   •

Monday morning I am instructed to go to Principal Scott's office as soon as I arrive at school.

Mr. Scott told me that the charges were dropped for the fight on Friday night because some of the students and Coach Williams had been interviewed and told the principal that I had nothing to do with the fight.

I want to tell Principal Scott that I fight all day, every day to survive.

I fight to eat.

I fight to have a place to sleep.

I fight for heat.

I fight for my life.

But I say nothing as he dismisses me for class. I need my daddy so bad. I need him to come and save me from Momma, because this is not getting any better. I need him to save Momma. Maybe it is time for me to go and live with Aunt Shirley. If I go over there,

I think she will come too, because she knows Aunt Shirley will tell Daddy that she is getting a check and I do not live with her. When Daddy started sending the checks to Granddaddy's house, she moved there. The checks can't go to Granddaddy's much longer anyway, because Aunt Shirley is going to buy that house and rent it out.

Hey, that's it! Momma goes where the checks go. All the way to class I think about how I am going to tell Momma that I am leaving. She might stay away a little while, but that will not last. She's going to follow that check.

"Hey, Nick. Hey, Paul," I say when I arrive at homeroom class ten minutes late. But they do not speak to me.

After roll call, the bell rings, and I try to catch up with them in the hall, but they keep walking when I get close to them.

"Hey, man, what's wrong with you guys?" I ask them when we get to math class.

"Man, we were trying to be your friends. Do you know those hood rats who jumped us at the dance Friday night?"

I cannot believe it. They are mad at me because I know those Lincoln High hoodlums. I think this is what Daddy calls guilty by association.

"Look, I know those two clowns, but they are not my friends. Five-O got me because I was wearing my old school jacket."

"Don't you know you're supposed to change jackets when you change schools, man?" Paul says.

"Cool, man, I'll get a new jacket." I wish I could tell them the truth. I wish I could tell them that this is the only jacket I have. All my other jackets are in Granddaddy's house, and I do not have money to buy a new jacket.

At lunchtime I reach into my pocket to check my messages and realize Jasmine's cell phone is gone. Momma must have taken it while I was asleep last night.

I can barely get through the day for thinking about Momma using that telephone all day. I have to forget about Momma and try to get through the next tennis tryouts.

"Hey, Coach," I say as I walk up to him on the court.

"Everything all right, Joseph?" Coach asks with a real look of concern on his face.

"I'm all right, Coach, and thanks for standing up for me on Friday."

"Just stay away from those guys, and let's play some tennis."

Well, he does not have to worry about me stay- ing away from them, because I heard today that

JOSEPH

the Cane twins got suspended for two weeks.

I am serving hard as April bounces around on the court trying to beat me again. Not today. I win fair and square. And I make the team! I want to go home and tell Momma, but she does not care about tennis and I am starting to feel like she does not care about me. But you had better believe she is going to ask about basketball practice before the week is out.

When I get home, she is sitting in the lobby of the shelter with this sad but almost crazy look on her face. It's that "I just finished smoking crack" look.

"What's wrong, Momma?" I ask.

"I lost your phone."

"That's not my phone. That's Jasmine's phone."

I do not want to deal with Momma's drama today, so I just walk away after that.

The wino who's sitting in the corner of the shelter door waves for me to come over to her.

"Your momma lying, kid. She sold your phone for twenty dollars to the drug dealer down the street."

I know that she is telling the truth, because Momma has that crack look again.

I run to the pay phone on the corner and use my last fifty cents to dial Jasmine's cell number.

"Who this?" some moron asks when he picks up.

What kind of English is that? I think. "I need that cell phone back, man," I say.

"This my phone now. Some woman sold it to me today and gave me a little something extra for cash. So unless you got fifty dollars, I am keeping this phone."

I hang up, because I do not want the dealer to trace the call back to a phone near the shelter.

I go to bed early without saying another word to Momma. I just keep thinking about how she sold our car last year and said that someone had stolen it.

Daddy had left Momma with a nice white Honda when he went to Raleigh. I came home from school one day and it was gone. A few days later I saw one of the drug dealers in the neighborhood driving the car. He parked at the drugstore, and I walked over to the car to get a closer look. It still had my book bag in the backseat.

"Sir, please don't get mad," I said to the dope dealer through his window. "I know I should not bother you, but that is my book bag in the backseat and I need it for school."

He looked up from rolling a joint and said, "Li'l man, you better get out of here."

The dude with him in the car said, "That's Betty's boy. Give him his book bag."

The dude just threw it out the window onto the ground. I never said a word to Momma about what happened at the drugstore. I guess she thought an angel brought my book bag back to me. Or she hadn't even known it was in the car at all.

After the money was gone from the sale of the car Momma cashed in all my savings bonds the day they matured. Anything for money. Anything not to work.

Anything for crack.

How am I going to tell Aunt Shirley about the phone?

CHAPTER SEVEN

I get to school early Tuesday morning to work on my tennis serve. Of course April is already on the court. No wonder she is so good.

We both practice our serves until the first bell rings.

I am getting dressed when I hear the principal paging me. When I get to the office, Aunt Shirley is there waiting for me. I thought it might have been Daddy, but I should have known it would be Aunt Shirley coming to find out who has Jasmine's telephone. At least, that is what I think she is here for.

"Hi, Aunt Shirley."

"Joseph, how are you?" she asks. She is standing with two teachers whom I do not recognize.

"Is something wrong?" I ask.

That is when I realize that the two women are not teachers; they are social workers. Aunt Shirley has finally followed through with her threats to Momma. I knew this day would come.

"Joseph," she says, "these women are from the Department of Social Services. I know you think you're old enough to know what is best for you, but your father and I disagree. These women are here to help you. All you have to do is tell them that you want to live with me and they will help you."

"I will get your cell phone back, Auntie," I say, trying to get out of this mess that Momma has caused.

Trying to save Momma from the authorities again.

"Oh, son, we are not here because your mother took the cell phone. I am not mad about that. I cannot sit back and let you live in that shelter. I want you to stay with me, Jasmine, and your Uncle Todd until your dad comes home."

"Can Momma come too?"

Aunt Shirley looks at me like she is surprised.

"I am all she has, Auntie, and I do not want to leave her."

"She can come if she wants to, but you have to. Your daddy and I will give you a few more nights at that shelter. That's it."

"Can I please be excused for class?"

The principal excuses me and I do not hear a word the teachers say all day. I want the day to end so that I can get home and tell Momma that she had better straighten up before the social workers take me away from her. This time they are serious. I really do want to go with my aunt; I just want Momma to come too. I have to convince her to come and live with Aunt Shirley and me tomorrow.

"See you tomorrow," I call to Jade, who is a new girl on the bus. She is so pretty, but I do not want to talk to her too much because she might ask too many questions. I do not want Jade or Melanie to know I live in the shelter. Melanie does not ask me too much, and she does not know that I catch the poor folks' bus back to the hood.

"Bye, Joseph," Jade says, giving me a big smile.

I go into a grocery store to make sure the bus is gone. I want to make sure that Jade does not see me even going in the direction of the shelter. The men in the store are doing what they do every single day. They're sitting around talking about everything under the sun. Mainly talking is the storeowner, Mr. Webb. He loves good gossip. He and Mr. Felix are really gossiping about something hot today.

"Hey, Joseph," Mr. Webb says as he rings up my Skittles.

"Hey, Mr. Webb," I say as I walk toward the door.

He is laughing real hard about something.

"Yeah," Mr. Felix says. "I told that tramp who lives at the shelter to get out of here. She was trying to sell herself. She ain't got no dignity. She will do anything for crack."

Another man joins in. "She is something all right. She tried to sell me a cell phone yesterday."

I stop at the door. They are talking about Momma!

"She sold the phone for crack to that boy of Melba's, and then she tried to use her body to get the phone back," Mr. Felix continues. I feel like someone has pulled my insides out of my body. I feel empty. I think I am going to throw up.

I drop my book bag and run over to Mr. Felix. I do not remember hitting him, but I do. I hit him several times before Mr. Webb grabs me. Then I start hitting Mr. Webb.

"What is wrong with you, boy?" he shouts.

"My momma, my momma!"

"What about your momma, boy?"

Then Mr. Webb realizes what is going on. No man has looked at me like that since Granddaddy died.

"Son, son, is Betty your momma?"

"Yes, sir," I say as I try to look at him real mean. But the tears just come out instead. He had no way of knowing who Momma is, because it is unlikely she is going for an afternoon walk with me.

Mr. Webb holds on to me like I am his child.

Rocking me back and forth in his arms like he loves me.

Mr. Felix picks up his hat. "Get some help for the boy," he says to Mr. Webb, and he pats me on the back. "Sorry, child." I want to jump on him again, but I am too tired to fight anymore.

With my head hung low, I finally walk out of the store. When I turn the corner I see Momma sitting on the front porch of the shelter. I do not look at her.

"I got the phone back, dude," she yells as I walk past her.

I do not even want to think about what she did to get that phone back. I go up to our room and lie down on the bed, covering my head with the blanket that smells like Momma's cheap perfume. Even though it is cheap, I love the smell. It reminds me that I do still have something left of her that is good. I cannot stop crying.

Now Daddy is not the only man who knows my momma will do anything for money. Everyone on the block knows. Soon everyone in town will know. Maybe the whole world will know.

I fall asleep without eating the awful dinner that they serve in the soup kitchen downstairs.

CHAPTER EIGHT

"**Good morning, dude,**" Momma says when I wake up the next morning.

"Good morning, Momma," I say quietly as I gather up my blue washcloth, towel, and clothes to walk down the hall to take a shower. We have had hard times before, but this is the first time that we have lived in a shelter, and I have never had to share a shower with other people before.

The water wakes me up from what feels like a bad dream. Only I am not dreaming. This is our life.

I keep thinking about Momma in bed with some strange man. I still feel like I am going to throw up.

I slip out of the shelter without going back into the room to say good-bye to Momma. I do not want to face her again until after school. Not until after my math test.

My math teacher, Ms. Rowe, says I am a good math student and will do well in Trig with more tutoring from Paul. I do not know why I am so bad in math. Daddy said that was his favorite subject. I will just have to keep working hard because I want to go to college. Coach Williams says the only way to stay on his team is to make good grades. I hope Momma does not find out that basketball tryouts are next week, because she will start bugging me about basketball.

All day long I think about what the men at the corner store said about Momma yesterday.

It's not like I can talk about this with anyone. What do I do? Go up to Nick and Paul and say, "Hey, man, my momma sold her body to get enough money to get my phone back from a dope dealer"? I don't think so.

I make a seventy-five on my math test.

"Joseph," Ms. Rowe says when I see her later in the day. "Joseph, is there something wrong?"

"No, Ms. Rowe. Everything is cool, why?"

"Well, for starters, I know that you knew every answer on that test. How could you end up with a seventy-five?"

I do not answer her right away because I know that Aunt Shirley has already told the principal about Momma. One more bad report to the social worker and I will not have time to convince Momma to come and live with me and Aunt Shirley; they will just take me away and she will end up homeless and alone.

"Ms. Rowe, I'm just having a bad day. Can I go now so that I will not miss my bus?"

"Yes, you can go, Joseph. Next Monday you can take a makeup test. I know you know this material." She does not say anything else. She just looks at me like Aunt Shirley does when she knows that I am lying.

I barely get to the bus in time.

When I get back to the shelter, Momma is not sitting on the porch. She's asleep on the mattress. I try to wake her up until I see the wine bottle on the floor next to her. I guess she got some money from somewhere. Who knows?

I look at the cell phone and it has seven messages. Six are from Clarine and the seventh one is from Daddy.

"Son, it's Daddy. I will be home on Friday, October 1st. I will try to call you again tonight."

He is coming home. He will help us.

I sleep hard. Just knowing that Daddy is on the way home makes everything all right. Then I hear a scream down the hall.

"Momma?" I say, sitting straight up on the mattress.

She is not beside me.

Forgetting to put on my jeans, I run to the door in my boxer shorts, but I can't get out of my room. Smoke is filling the hallway.

I can suddenly hear Ms. Lynn, who shares the room next door with her six children, yelling from outside for me to jump out of the window. I run to the window.

"Ms. Lynn, where's my momma?"

"Outside. Now jump, boy!"

I peer into the dark through the smoke and see Momma standing near the curb. She's screaming too. "Jump! Jump!"

I wrap my Lincoln High jacket around my fist and break the window. Grabbing a few things from the room, I throw them out the window. I am so scared, but I jump down from the second-floor window and land at the feet of Ms. Lynn.

Momma just stands there looking like a madwoman.

The police help us all into their patrol cars and drive us to a larger shelter over on Linden Street. Ms. Lynn keeps whispering to Momma, and I can tell that Ms. Lynn is really angry. I move over closer to hear what she is saying.

"If any of my children had been hurt, I would have turned you in, woman," Ms. Lynn says as she rolls her eyes at Momma and pulls her baby girl Keidra away from Momma.

Oh God, Momma started the fire.

• • •

When we get inside the new shelter, I pull Momma by the arm to get her away from the other homeless people.

"Please tell me that you did not start that fire, Momma." I shake her arm hard.

Before she can answer, Five-O is standing behind me.

"Miss, we have to ask you a few questions."

Momma starts to throw one of her tantrums. The kind she throws when she is mad at Daddy. "What do you want to ask me?" She points her finger at the officer, looking wild. "I did not start that fire."

"Shut up, Momma. We need to call Aunt Shirley."

"Sorry, Miss, but you will have to come with us to the police station."

I do not say anything as they drag Momma off, kicking and screaming.

"Where are they taking my momma?" I ask Ms. Lynn.

She just looks at me and says, "To jail, I hope."

That hurts because Ms. Lynn has always liked me and tried to be nice to Momma. But everyone is tired of Momma.

I ask the shelter manager if I can use the phone to call Aunt Shirley.

Half-asleep, my aunt answers the telephone.

"Aunt Shirley, get here quick. Five-O just took Momma to jail."

"Jail! Where are you?"

"I don't know. The shelter burned down and they moved us to another one."

"Burned down!" Aunt Shirley screams into the telephone.

"It's gone, Auntie. There was a fire tonight. I'll get the name of this shelter from someone who lives here," I say as Aunt Shirley screams for Jasmine to turn on her laptop to Google directions to the new shelter.

"My poor nephew!" she screams into the phone.

It takes her a few moments to ask about Momma. "Why did they take Betty?" she finally asks.

"They think she started the fire."

"Oh God, is anyone hurt?"

Before I can answer, Jasmine takes the telephone from her momma.

"What's the name of the shelter?" she asks.

"Hey, sir, what's the name of this place?" I ask the white man sitting at the front desk.

"King's Homeless Shelter on Fifth and Linden Street," he says like he really does not want to be bothered.

"I heard him. We'll be right there," my cousin says as she hangs up on me.

I sit in the corner and watch as the homeless try to figure out if they are going to be able to spend the night at this shelter. The Red Cross is trying to place the people who cannot stay here. This shelter is full now, thanks to Momma.

All the people from the old shelter look at me with pitying stares and try not to say bad things about Momma. But they hate her now, just like most people do.

Aunt Shirley and Jasmine are at the shelter within twenty minutes. Aunt Shirley is still wearing her pajamas with a coat over them. We hug as she talks to Ms. Lynn.

"Miss, can you tell me what happened?"

"Not in front of the child," Ms. Lynn whispers, and nods in my direction.

"I'm sorry for what I said to you earlier, Joseph," Ms. Lynn says as she walks away with my aunt.

The one thing that I notice about other mothers is they are always trying to protect me from Momma. Momma has always said any and everything in front of me. Whatever she wants to say about Daddy, she just yells it out loud. Whatever she wants me to know that she thinks will hurt my relationship with him just comes out of her mouth. What she does not say to me about my daddy, she will say on the telephone to Clarine when I am around so that I can hear it.

Her love/hate feelings for Daddy got us in this mess.

I can read Ms. Lynn's lips as she is talking to Aunt Shirley.

"Keep the boy," she says.

That's what Granddaddy would always say to Aunt Shirley. And what he always said to Daddy.

"Are we going to the police station?" I ask my aunt.

"No, we are not. I'm taking you and Jasmine home. I am going to the police station."

No one says a word as we drive out of the bad neighborhood into the suburbs to Aunt Shirley's beautiful house on the hill.

"Put some sheets on the bed in the guest room," Aunt Shirley says to Jasmine as my cousin and I get out of the car.

"What is going to happen to Momma?" I ask Aunt Shirley, but she is already pulling out of the driveway.

"When is the last time you ate?" Jasmine asks as I eat the soup that Aunt Shirley left in the refrigerator.

"Lunchtime," I answer as I turn the bowl up to my mouth to get the last drop of soup.

"Do you think they're going to keep Momma all night?" I ask my cousin when I lower the bowl to the table.

"I do not know, cousin. Momma is a good attorney. If anyone can get her out, Momma can." Jasmine kisses me on the forehead and starts to go upstairs. "Go to bed after you eat all you want. I have two tests in the morning."

I go into the den and lie on the couch. This room is larger than the whole entire shelter that Momma and I were living in. I turn on the TV and try to wait up for Aunt Shirley and Momma.

The sunshine wakes me up the next morning.

"Where's Momma?" I ask as Aunt Shirley walks through the den going to the kitchen.

"Upstairs, asleep. They couldn't keep her because there are no witnesses who actually saw her set the fire. There were a few people who said they saw her smoking in the hallway earlier, but that is not enough to arrest. The police are doing an investigation." Aunt

Shirley stops in front of the TV that I left playing all night.

"Did you see your mother smoking?" she asks, looking down into my eyes as if she will be able to know if I lie to her.

"No, Aunt Shirley. I did not see her smoking last night. I was asleep."

"Yo, Shirley, you better leave my boy alone," Momma yells as she stumbles down the stairs in the same clothes she had on yesterday. She smells of smoke.

"Girl, if you don't get back up those steps with all of that drama . . . ," Aunt Shirley threatens. "It's time for Joseph to take a shower and go to school. Leave him be."

They start arguing again.

I go upstairs and find a bag from Wal-Mart lying on the bed in the guest room. I cannot believe it.

Aunt Shirley has gone to the only open-all-night store and bought me jeans and T-shirts for school. She has even laid out Uncle Todd's North Carolina State jacket on the bed for me to wear. I pick it up and smell his Armani cologne.

"It's okay to wear it, son."

I turn around and there he is. My Uncle Todd in his pilot's uniform, standing in the doorway.

"Sorry I wasn't here for you last night, Joseph. I just flew in from San Francisco."

"It's all right, Uncle. I know you want to help."

"I do want to help, and your aunt does too. We want you guys to stay here."

"Momma too?" I ask, knowing that they really do not want her here.

"Yes, your momma, too," Uncle Todd says as he takes the jacket, holding it out to see if it will fit me.

The jacket looks so cool. Wait until Paul and Nick see me in this.

"Now, throw away those clothes from the shelter. They stink from the smoke. I'll drive you to school so I can come home and hit the sack before going to the golf course."

Uncle Todd puts the jacket back on the bed. "Oh, and you can keep the jacket," he says, leaving the room.

I cannot believe my ears. It is for me to keep. Now I do not have to wear that Lincoln jacket anymore. Cool!

You can hear a pin drop at the table as everyone eats the good breakfast that Aunt Shirley has cooked. Momma did not want to come down to eat, but I know she is just as hungry as I am. Then we all kiss good-bye like a real family.

Momma just sits in her room upstairs as Aunt

Shirley gets her briefcase, ready to leave the house with Jasmine. I hold Momma's right hand tight as she reaches for her cigarettes with the other hand as soon as Aunt Shirley turns her back. I know they will be fighting again if Aunt Shirley turns around. But Aunt Shirley does not have to see Momma. She knows her sister well enough. Without turning around, she says, "No smoking in the house, Betty."

Momma hisses, "Shut up, bossy."

Jasmine and I laugh as we walk out the door with my aunt and uncle. Uncle Todd will drop me off, and Jasmine is driving herself to class in her new Volkswagen. How cool is that?

Momma is probably glad that we are all gone so that she can do as she pleases all day in that fancy house.

CHAPTER NINE

Uncle Todd picks me up after school and we drive off as Nick and Paul give each other a high five, because Uncle Todd is driving a cool white Benz 500.

"Where's Momma?" I ask.

"I guess she's at home, son. I've been on the golf course all day."

"All day?" I ask.

"Yes, all day. I ended up going there after I dropped you off this morning, and I forgot I was sleepy when I got on the golf course. When you get real good at tennis you will be doing the same thing. Playing all the time. Except when you're not studying, of course."

Uncle Todd gets this serious look on his face. The look Aunt Shirley gets when she is getting ready to talk about Momma.

"I know you love your momma, son, but you really have to look at her situation. She has a few problems, and she needs help. We want her to go to rehab."

"She's not going to go on her own," I tell Uncle Todd.

"Okay, then what do you think we should do with her in the shape that she is in?"

"What shape? She is not a monster!"

"No need to get upset. And, no, she is not a monster, but she *is* an addict and she needs help," Uncle Todd says as he pulls into the driveway.

"Uncle Todd, Momma is not going to stay in rehab. She is going to do drugs until they kill her."

"That's right. The drugs *will* kill her if she does not get help. But we can help her. Don't you want her to get help?"

"Yes, sir. I do."

"Good. I will talk about this with Aunt Shirley. She has been looking into treatment centers all day. But this is for the adults to handle. You are too young to handle this on your own. When your daddy gets here, we will get this process started."

It will take more than Daddy coming home to get Momma into rehab, I am thinking as we get out of the car and go inside. Aunt Shirley is not home from work, and Jasmine is studying as usual.

"Hey, Momma," I say as she breaks away long enough from the telephone conversation she is having to barely kiss me.

She is happy that she is in a place where she can talk to Clarine. Clarine has been in rehab more times than Momma, and she cannot keep a job either. Every car she has ever owned was repossessed, and she had more problems than Momma has, but their conversations are still always about Uncle Ed and Daddy. They talk about how "no-good" Uncle Ed is because he dumped Clarine and married someone who was not changing jobs every six months and cussing out each boss on her way out the door.

I can tell from their conversation that they are thinking about getting a place together. I hope not! Clarine lived with us for a week just after Daddy left. I guess she was in between boyfriends. One night I heard voices and went downstairs to see what was going on. Clarine had convinced some guy to buy them his-and-hers red BMWs. But Clarine was supposed to make the payments on her car. Of course, she did not, and the guy was at our house to collect his money or the car. When she wouldn't give him the keys, he pulled out a gun and put it in her mouth. The only reason that man did not kill her was he saw my reflection in the hallway mirror. I was watching the whole thing go down, and I felt like I was watching a bad movie. I will never forget the feeling that I had saved her life.

"I got children of my own. Get out of here while you can, boy," the man said to me as he walked out the door. Momma slept through the whole thing.

I never saw him again, but he found my daddy and told him about Clarine and Momma doing drugs. He apologized to Daddy for what he had done with me in the house. Daddy did not want to hear it, and he told him to never set foot in that house again.

Daddy came to the house the next day. But Momma and Clarine called the police and told them that Daddy was trespassing. I cannot believe Momma is thinking about moving in with this woman again.

It became too much for Daddy to try to see me at Momma's, and he started coming to school to visit me. Sometimes he would be waiting in the parking lot with breakfast when my bus pulled up.

I would sit there with him and talk until the bell rang. Sometimes we sat there and did not say a word.

"Hey, Momma," I say for the second time, trying to get her to stop talking to someone who is worse off than she is.

I can hear Clarine screaming in the telephone. "Hey, dude!" That's the way she talks to me too, like Momma does. "Hey, dude"—like we are the same age.

I give up and go into the kitchen to do my homework while Momma finishes her baby mama drama conversation. When Aunt Shirley comes home, she changes clothes and starts to prepare dinner. I can smell the smothered chicken all over the house. It has been so long since I came home to a hot meal. The table is set so nice. Just like those tables on TV.

Momma does not even bother to help Aunt Shirley with dinner. She is back on the telephone with Clarine. Aunt Shirley has no patience for Momma's craziness and she finally has enough of Momma's laughing and talking with Clarine about her check from Daddy being late.

"Girl, hang up that phone and spend some time with your son."

I think Momma was hanging around on the phone just waiting for Aunt Shirley to say something so the yelling can start again. But not with Uncle Todd in the house. He is not going to listen to that mess.

"Both of you shut up! The children are trying to study."

I am so happy that Uncle Todd makes them stop fussing. I want to have dinner like a real family.

Momma rolls her eyes at Uncle Todd and pops her chewing gum really loud. "Talk to you later, Clarine," she says as she hangs up the phone.

CHAPTER TEN

We have been living here for a whole week now and the drama with Momma is not as bad as it was when we first got here. I have clean sheets on the bed, good food, and a ride to school every day.

Friday comes and then Momma goes back to her old ways. She is off to happy hour. When I get home from tennis practice she is all dressed in Aunt Shirley's clothes with her hair in a French roll or some fancy do. Aunt Shirley ignores her, even though everything she is wearing is Aunt Shirley's.

She must be really sick of Momma to let her leave here in her designer stuff. Poor Momma, she is too big for Aunt Shirley's clothes, and she has on every piece of jewelry that she owns. It's all fake jewelry, but you had better not tell Momma that.

No one says a word as she walks out the door, leaving me with my family. I think they are just glad that she is not going to be home to ruin dinner again tonight. I must admit that I am glad she is leaving too.

Uncle Todd and I watch TV like I used to with Daddy. At midnight he goes to bed, and I stay up and play video games with Jasmine until she falls asleep on the couch.

I had all kinds of toys and video games when Daddy lived with us. One by one Momma pawned everything away, including my bible.

At 2 a.m. Momma is still not home. I begin to

worry, because I thought she might come in early so that she would not have to hear Aunt Shirley fussing at her.

I finally fall asleep too, only to wake up at four o'clock and find Momma's bed still empty.

At six o'clock she is still not home. I cannot worry about her today, because my first tennis match with the team is today. Maybe it is good she is not going with me to school. It will not take long for the parents and Coach Williams to start disliking her too.

I put on the nice jeans that my aunt and uncle bought me. Uncle Todd has filled my closet with T-shirts of different sports teams from all over the country. It is so nice not to have to search through used clothes at the homeless shelter anymore.

More than anything, Daddy is e-mailing me all the time as he prepares to come back to the States.

He knows that Momma is hanging out and that we are living with Auntie. He said he is going to straighten all of this out when he comes home.

With my tennis clothes in my new gym bag and my racquet, I follow Uncle Todd to the garage after a light breakfast. Uncle Todd said I should never eat heavily before a match.

When Uncle Todd and I open the garage door, we see Momma sitting in his Benz with some guy we have never seen before. Uncle Todd looks at the garage door and loses his mind when he realizes that they have broken into his garage and spent the night in his car.

"Man, what the hell are you doing in my garage?" Uncle Todd shouts as he grabs the tennis racquet out of my hand.

"Just hanging out with my baby," the stranger says as he gets out of the car and starts to walk backward. I have never seen Uncle Todd so mad before.

Aunt Shirley comes out to the garage to see what is going on. "Betty, I *know* you did not sleep in the garage with this man all night."

"Child, I am not thinking about you," Momma says, blowing the man a kiss. "I am grown. You best get your uppity tail back inside." Then Momma blows the man another kiss.

"What kind of mother *are* you?" Aunt Shirley says.

"Are you calling me a bad mother?" Momma asks, as if she does not already know the answer to that question.

I feel like I am on *The Jerry Springer Show.*

Jasmine comes to the door in her pj's. Lord, the child is crying again.

Aunt Shirley walks down the garage steps like she is on *The Jerry Springer Show* too.

"Yes, you are a bad mother. You are the worst of the worst."

"Is that right?" Momma barks. "If that is the case, you keep Joseph." She turns to me and says, "Momma loves you, Joseph baby, but I am not wanted here."

"That's not true, Momma," I say. "They want to help you. They are going to help you get in rehab next week." I did not mean for that to come out so fast.

"Rehab! I ain't going to no damn rehab."

Then Momma yells out to the man she has spent the night with, who is halfway down the block already, "Wait up, baby, my folks don't want me here. Now they are trying to send me to rehab."

I do not know why, but my breakfast starts to come back up all over Uncle Todd's uniform.

"It's all right, son, it's all right," Uncle Todd says as Jasmine rubs my back.

Aunt Shirley yells at Momma. "Shame on you, girl. Shame on you!"

"There goes the neighborhood," Aunt Shirley says as she pulls herself together.

Now everyone on this street knows that Momma is a crackhead.

Uncle Todd is holding me up as I puke all over his Benz.

Once again Momma has found someone else to put before me. My guess is she was planning to leave anyway. She is going to use this jerk to get herself a new address to get her illegal welfare checks, so she will not need Aunt Shirley anymore.

It hurts so bad to watch Momma leave with that man. A man who does not even have a car. They walk down the street arm in arm.

I try to run out of the garage to stop her, but Uncle Todd grabs my arm. "Son, let her go. She'll be back. But let her go for now."

Uncle Todd puts on a clean suit in a hurry while I change clothes too. We all jump into Aunt Shirley's car and rush over to Dulles for my tennis match. I'm getting excited now.

I cannot believe that all these people are here to support their kids on a Saturday morning.

What a match! Not only did we win, but I also played a good game and was named Best Player today.

"Good game, Joseph," Coach Williams says, and Melanie runs over to give me a hug.

Jasmine and Aunt Shirley are looking at Melanie like I am not supposed to have a female friend.

Oh no, Jade is coming over now too!

Paul and Nick think this is funny. "You cornered,

man," Paul says with a big laugh. "You got two chicks digging you."

I do not have two chicks, but it is nice to have friends.

CHAPTER ELEVEN

More than a week has passed, and I still have not heard one word from Momma. The only thing that keeps me going is Daddy. He and I talk every time he can get a call through to me. Now that I am at Aunt Shirley's, I check my e-mail all the time, and Daddy is always sending me messages, trying to keep my spirits high.

I miss Momma, but I am doing so much better without having to deal with her drugs and men every day. I just pray that she is okay.

Aunt Shirley saw Ms. Monet at the spa yesterday,

and she told my aunt that Momma finally called her trying to get her to let her use Ms. Monet's address to make sure I stayed in the same school. When Ms. Monet told Momma that she knew I was living with Aunt Shirley, Momma asked to borrow some money. That was the real reason she had called in the first place. Ms. Monet told her no and hung up. Ms. Monet is not going to take that abuse. But she assured Aunt Shirley that Momma is doing okay because she is still cussing out anyone who will let her.

I have decided not to take it anymore either. I want Momma to come back to us and get some help, but if she does not, I am staying here.

I just got another e-mail from Daddy.

Hi, Son,

How are you? I am well. I have good news and bad

news for you. The good news is I am still coming home on Friday. The bad news is I can only stay one week. We can get a hotel, or Shirley has offered me a room at the house with you guys.

Maybe we can drive down to Raleigh to visit your family. The fall is a good time to go fishing. Yep, let's go fishing.

I know you are worried about your momma, but your aunt says she is living with Clarine. That can't be good, but what can we do?

Stay strong, and I will see you in a few days.

Love,

Daddy

That e-mail makes me sick to my stomach all over again. "Oh, god, Momma is starting to physically make me sick." The thought of Momma living with Clarine is worse than her living with a stranger. Or did Aunt Shirley tell Daddy that so he would not know Momma had run off with another man? Or maybe he got the news from Uncle Todd. I hope Momma is not with Clarine, because Clarine is always making some man mad. She lives in danger because she uses men to get what she wants. She used her body to get cars, furniture from Havertys, you name it. She is always calling the police after someone beats her or threatens to beat her. Now if Momma's over there with Clarine, Momma will be caught in the middle of that drama, as if she does not have enough of her own.

I pray hard and try not to think about how Momma is living.

I have been going to tennis practice this week, and I really want to keep doing well. Uncle Todd bought me a new racquet because I was using one that belongs to the school. Daddy sent me an e-mail this morning that he will see me at my aunt's house tonight.

I can hardly sit in my seat at school, just knowing that Daddy will be home later.

When the last bell rings, I run outside, expecting Uncle Todd to be there waiting for me. But he is not here. We are supposed to go to Belk's to get me a new suit for church with the money Daddy sent to Aunt Shirley, and then come back for tennis practice.

Paul and Nick come outside and join me.

"What's up, man? You're not talking much today," Nick says.

"I'm cool. I can't wait for my dad to get home from Iraq."

"Iraq! Guy, you are full of surprises," Paul exclaims. "You never mentioned your daddy is over there. My oldest brother is there too."

"I think everybody in this school knows at least one person in Iraq," Nick says as my mind wanders and I wonder where my uncle could be. He is never late.

Maybe he does not want me to stay with him anymore, I think as I look around.

"Looking for someone?" a deep voice says from behind me.

It's my daddy. In full uniform.

"I came straight from the airport," he says. "My rental car is over there. Come on, son."

I do not care what the guys think. I fall into Daddy's arms and cry. Daddy is crying too.

Paul and Nick look real happy as they check out my daddy and all the medals on his uniform.

Ms. Rowe, who is on bus duty, walks over to us.

"You must be Joseph's father," she says with a smile on her face.

"Yes, I am." Daddy answers like he is really proud.

"He's a good boy and a good student. I'm glad that you're home to help him out."

Daddy does not ask Ms. Rowe what she means. He has heard this sort of thing so many times before from so many teachers that he knows she must have had her run-in with Momma. Or at least she has heard about her. Daddy shakes her hand and thanks her for caring about me.

"Can you stay for my tennis practice, Daddy?"

"Yes, I can, son. Todd told me he was supposed to take you shopping, but we can do that later. I want to talk to a few of your teachers, too."

After he walks around the school to talk to the few teachers who are still in their classrooms late on a Friday, Daddy sits on the sidelines with Paul and watches as Nick and I play tennis.

For a while, I can see Daddy talking to Coach

Williams. I hope Coach is telling him good stuff about me.

My daddy is funny as he yells directions over to me. "A little lower, son!"

I love every word that he yells. I am just so glad that he is home.

After tennis practice, I say good-bye to Nick and Paul, and Daddy and I go to the sushi restaurant on McConnell Road, where we sit for hours.

"Daddy, I still have not heard from Momma," I say after a while.

Daddy does not say anything at first. Then he says, "Son, one day you will be a fine man. Right now you are a young man and not responsible for your momma or for me. We are supposed to be responsible for *you*. Your momma always finds a way to survive. She is doing what she wants to do. This is not the first time she has left you, and it may not be the last."

I want to defend her, but I don't. My daddy has never talked bad about her the way she talks bad about him. I know he has reached his breaking point with her.

"I am only here for a week," he continues. "I have to report to Fort McPherson in Atlanta next Monday. We will try to help your momma, but you are my primary responsibility. I need you to promise me that you will not leave your aunt Shirley's house no matter what happens with your momma."

I do not really want to make that promise, because I hope Momma will get herself together and we can have a home together again one day.

"You have to promise me that, son."

"I promise," I say as I finish my food.

When we get home, Aunt Shirley and the whole family are so glad to see Daddy. I can tell that the grown-ups want me and Jasmine to get lost, though, so they can talk to Daddy privately about Momma.

I am not trying to eavesdrop, but I overhear Aunt Shirley and Daddy talking about Momma one night when they think I am watching TV in the den.

"Peter, you get out of that army as fast as you can. I love my sister, but she is not getting any better. She can only hold a job for a few weeks and then she is back to her old self. No work, no money, and lying."

My daddy tries to show some compassion, but it is clear that his concern is for me.

"Shirley, I have six more months in the army. If you can keep my boy until I return, it would be best for him. The money I was sending to Betty I will continue to send to you. Let her take me to court, and that will give me a second chance to tell the

JOSEPH

judge about her drug addiction. I can't save her, but
I can save my son."

That will smoke Momma out of her hiding with
Clarine, I am thinking as I listen. A while ago I saw
Momma filling out a change of address for her mail
to come here and not to Granddaddy's place. The
one sure way to get Momma's attention is not to
send her that check at all.

When she goes to Granddaddy's old mailbox
and the money is not there, she will come running
over here to Aunt Shirley's. She should not still be
receiving mail at that house anyway.

All week I hang out with my daddy before and
after school. He tries not to talk about what is going
on in this war, but I know he is scared. I can hear him
walking around in the room next to me during the
night. He is scared that he will have to leave Atlanta
and go back to Iraq.

153

In the afternoons, Daddy comes to school and watches me at tennis practice.

"Good job, boy," he yells from the sidelines. That makes me proud.

Today is Friday, and Daddy has decided to spend most of the day at school talking to my teachers. He does something that he would not have done a few years ago. Today Daddy tells the principal and my coach and teachers all about Momma and her drugs. That bothers me, but I know that he is upset about having to leave me again, and he wants these people to know what is happening with me.

As if I was born to make sure that she receives her check each month, Momma is at Aunt Shirley's when Daddy and I get home this Friday evening.

"Hey, Momma, I have a tennis match tomorrow. Please come," I say as I jump out of the car and run over to her. She sits on the front porch, using Aunt Shirley's cordless phone. Of course she is talking to the other professional baby mama, telling her how she and Aunt Shirley had it out with each other earlier today. I am glad that I was at school.

"Here he comes, girl. I got to go," Momma says. "Hey, dude, go inside. I need to talk to your daddy."

She has not seen me in more than two weeks, and she is so concerned about her check that she forgets to hug me.

"Go inside, Joseph," Daddy says to me.

"I did not get my check, Peter," Momma says.

"Hello to you, too, Betty. Did you hear your son ask you about his tennis match?"

"Tennis! He ain't Venus and Serena Williams! He better be thinking about basketball. I told that boy a thousand times and he is still playing tennis like a fool."

I push my bedroom window up higher so I can hear them. Aunt Shirley comes upstairs to my room. "Get out of that window," she says. "What your parents talk about is not for your young ears, dear heart."

She puts her hand on my shoulder and starts to close the window, but it's too late. I finally hear what Momma really thinks about Daddy and me.

"Look, I need my money, Peter. How you take care of Joseph is your business. If you were not trying to be such a big man, I would have had an abortion anyway when I got pregnant. You wanted him; I just wanted a husband and a house! So *you* take care of him."

So Momma really did not want me. She never did. I was just a way for her to hold on to Daddy. Just a way to keep money in her pocket.

Daddy starts yelling at her, but then he looks up and his eyes meet mine through the window. He looks past Momma like she is wind in the air.

"I am sorry that you heard that, son," he yells, as he starts to run into the house.

"I'm not," I say, and I pull my shoulder from under Aunt Shirley's arm and run down and out of the house, past Daddy and Momma. I do not know where I am going. I just have to get away from everyone.

I can still hear Momma yelling at Daddy when I'm down the street. "See what you done? Now your boy is mad at me. I ain't playing with you, Peter, I want my money!" Those are the last words I heard from her mouth, because I run as fast as I can to get out of the range of her voice.

Aunt Shirley runs behind me with no shoes on her feet. When she finally catches up with me two blocks away, she is out of breath and cries out, "Stop, honey, please stop!" I know her neighbors think we are a bunch of hood rats.

For two hours we sit on the curb and talk.

"Your daddy is a good man, and it may not seem like it, but your momma was a good person when she was young. She was my sister before she was your mother, and she was a good sister and friend. We did everything together. Her drug problems are so out of control now that we can no longer help her. She has to want to help herself. I feel like I don't know her anymore."

It has been a long time since I have seen Aunt Shirley show her love for Momma. She is so mad at Momma most of the time.

"I am so sorry that you had to hear all of that crazy mess come out of her mouth," Aunt Shirley continues.

"Is it true, Auntie? Is it true that she wanted to have an abortion?"

Aunt Shirley is silent for a minute.

"Oh, nephew, I do not know the answer to that question. Only your mother and God know that. I just know that you are here and your daddy and both of your families love you. We are so glad that you were born."

We hug for a long time.

We walk back to the house to find Daddy sitting on the porch with Uncle Todd.

"I can't speak for Betty. I just know that I want you, son."

That is all he says. It is enough. And then Daddy is hugging me like I am two years old.

The last morning that I have left with Daddy, we spend talking about everything. I sit on the bed and watch him dress. He looks so nice in his uniform.

"Daddy, tell me the truth. Momma never wanted me, huh?" I say as I help him to put his jacket on.

"I do not know the answer to that one, son. My answer is the same. I want you now and I have always wanted you, my son. No matter what she does with her life, you have a family."

I know that the conversation is closed when he hugs me.

Daddy drives me to school and we talk about happier times.

"Hey, Daddy, do you remember that time when we went fishing and I thought we could eat the fish right off the pole?"

"That's hard to forget, boy. I'm glad that I stopped you. We would still be sitting at the hospital."

We laugh all the way to school.

I stand outside the school grounds until Daddy's rental car is completely out of sight.

We have said good-bye again.

For now.

CHAPTER TWELVE

All the things I thought were bad in life became worse when I learned Momma never wanted me. I was nothing more than an accident. Then I became a paycheck and Momma's pawn to make my daddy miserable. On top of that, Momma is a crackhead.

I do not know what I am going to do now. I do not know how to stop loving her. I do not think I am supposed to stop. I just cannot let her destroy my life, like she is destroying her own.

"Hey, man," a voice calls from behind me as I am walking to my homeroom class.

I turn around and it is that hoodlum, Arthur Cane. I know better than to get caught up with this guy.

"Hi, Arthur," I say, making sure that I don't stop walking. He knows that I do not want to be bothered with him, but he is the type of guy who does not like rejection.

"Want to shoot some ball after school?" he asks. He is just waiting for me to say no so that he can pick a fight.

"No, man, I have tennis practice today. I'll catch you some other time."

"Such a little girl," Arthur says as I walk away.

I want to turn around and take out all of my anger toward Momma on him, but I do not. I think about my promises to Daddy and the promise I made to Granddaddy. I promised them that I would always avoid trouble.

Arthur yells out "Sissy" a few times, but I do not pay him any attention as the few kids who are in the hall laugh at me. Nick and Paul catch up with me.

"Don't pay him any mind, man. He and his brother will be kicked out of here again before you know it," Paul says.

But calling me a sissy is not enough for Arthur. He comes into my homeroom class later.

"Hey, man, what's the deal? You think that you too good to be with the Lincoln boys?"

I try not to look at him as I take my seat.

"Man, don't ignore me. You aren't any better than me."

Over and over he calls me names as I try to ignore him. I am doing okay until I feel his right fist coming down on my eye and the whole class falls silent.

I do not remember much after that. Just the girls screaming and the boys egging us on. Melanie is screaming for us to stop as Paul and Nick try to help break up the fight.

I am definitely winning, but I do not even know why I am fighting this guy. The security guard finally arrives and pulls us apart.

Only a few months at my new school and I am already in trouble twice with the same guys from Lincoln.

"Looks as though you boys think you are still at Lincoln," Mr. Scott says as he writes up the detention slips. "Three days at home should do it for you both." He never even looks up. Arthur just got back to school after being suspended from his last fight and Principal Scott is simply not in the mood for the guys from the other side of the track bringing trouble to Dulles.

I am ashamed when I call Aunt Shirley. She must be in court because she is not answering, so I leave her a voice message.

Sitting on the bench in the principal's office waiting for Aunt Shirley feels like forever. She finally arrives and does not look at me. After she talks with Principal Scott for a few minutes, she waves her hand for me to come with her. "Are you hungry?" she asks as she pulls out of the school parking lot.

"Yes, ma'am, I am hungry."

"Good, because I want you to be sitting down when I am talking to you."

She pulls into Mr. Burger's and gets out of the car first.

I follow her inside, where she lets me order whatever I want. I know she is getting ready to put me on punishment, but at least I will have a full stomach.

"Son, I know your life has not been easy, but Uncle Todd and I will not tolerate you misbehaving in school. After all the talks your Daddy, Todd, and I have had with you, why would you do this?"

"It wasn't my fault. Arthur hit me first."

"Well, you were there and you did not walk away, so it is your fault."

I sit there and listen to her as she tells me I am grounded for a month. "This is for your own good."

"I know, Auntie."

No TV, no movies, nothing. Just school, church, and tennis.

When she finishes, she looks at me with Granddaddy's eyes and says, "Your momma called today."

"She did?"

"Yes, she wants you to go live with her in a rooming house not far from the old shelter. She said she does not want to live with Clarine because Clarine has had another baby."

That is no surprise about Clarine. Another baby means another support check from some guy.

"Is Momma okay?" I ask.

"Yes, she is all right, but not enough for you to live with her. You would have to go back to Lincoln and that is not the right thing for you to do, son. This is her number. You call her if you think you should call her. That's up to you, but you have to stay with us until Peter comes back."

I do not say anything as we finish eating.

Finally, Aunt Shirley says, "Now, I have to go back to work for a few hours. You go home and clean up the house from top to bottom."

"But the maid is coming tomorrow," I say.

"She was coming, but now you will be the maid for the next month. I will not tolerate you acting up in school. So go home and start cleaning."

She drives me home and leaves me standing at the curb in front of the house.

After I finish cleaning my room, I clean the room that Momma was sleeping in when she was here. She didn't even try to keep this room clean. The broom hits a box under the bed.

There must be a thousand pieces of tape on the box.

When I open the box I get that sick feeling in my stomach again.

Bills, bills, and more bills. All in my name.

I can't believe it.

I look at the address. No wonder Momma is running over to Granddaddy's house to get the mail all the time.

"Joseph, where are you?" It is Jasmine, home from school.

I have been sitting for over an hour in the same spot on the bed, going through all the late notices and letters from bill collectors addressed to me.

"Up here," I yell.

"What's wrong, cousin?" Jasmine asks. "What are you looking at?"

"Bills! Bills that my momma put in my name. Unpaid bills! My credit is ruined before I even get my first job."

I look at her as she dials the phone. "No, do not tell Aunt Shirley. Surely Momma will go back to jail."

Jasmine puts down the phone and hugs me.

We sit in the same spot for another hour.

CHAPTER THIRTEEN

I never say a word to my Aunt and Uncle about the bills under Momma's bed and I wonder how long it will take Jasmine to tell on Momma. I just get up every day and clean the house before going to school. I am tired, but it almost feels good to have someone that cares about me enough to put me on punishment.

Daddy calls or e-mails me in his every free moment.

Dear Son,

How are you? I hope that you are well. I got your e-mail about the fight, and I am disappointed that you did not walk away. Sometimes, son, walking away is the only way out.

Still have not heard from your momma? Try not to worry about her, and do not worry about me.

It is tough here at Fort McPherson, but nothing like Iraq. Here you just live with the fear of having to go back over there. In Iraq you are trying to stay alive.

How are your grades? How's tennis? How's Melanie? I can tell that you like that girl. She is nice. That is the kind of girl a father wants his son to bring home.

Love,

Daddy

I guess Aunt Shirley didn't tell him about that phone call from Momma. I do not want to upset him, so I write him back and never mention her. What can I say about her, anyway? I cannot tell him that she has a gold card in my name.

> Dear Daddy,
>
> How are you? I am well and I miss you.
>
> Everyone is treating me really nice, and I love tennis. I am becoming a real tennis champ and, boy, do I wish you were here to check me out.
>
> Yeah, I like Melanie. She is nice, Dad, and she makes good grades. I think I will marry her! Just kidding. . . .
>
> Your son,
>
> Joseph

This Friday the whole school shows up for the tennis match.

I am a little nervous at first, but I hear some people in the stands yelling my name. All dressed in our school colors, it is Ms. Monet, Valerie, Uncle Todd, Jasmine, Paul, Melanie, Jade, and Aunt Shirley. Everyone.

As mad as I am at Momma, I keep looking for her face in the crowd. I think of the smell of her cheap perfume. Then I think about the drugs, the cigarettes, the illegal checks, and my ruined credit.

I close my eyes and say a prayer.

God hears me.

We win the tennis match.

Life isn't getting any easier for Joseph Flood,
but he still hasn't lost hope. . . .

Turn the page for the first chapter of
JOSEPH'S GRACE, the sequel to JOSEPH.

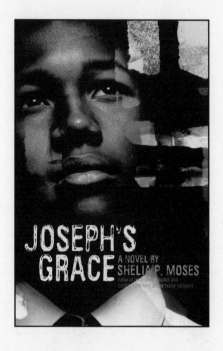

Available January 2011
from Margaret K. McElderry Books

"Amazzzzzzing Grace, how sweet the sound that saved a wretch like me. I once was lost but now I'm found; Wazzzzzzzzz blind, but now I seeeee." Miss Novella sings as everyone screams and cries at my cousin Jasmine's funeral.

"Help me Jesus," she says, and makes her way back to her seat in the choir stand after singing and shouting all over the place.

"Help me, Lord. Help me," she says between verses as Miss Fitten fans her with the paper fan that has a picture of Martin Luther King Jr. and his family on it. Miss Fitten is crying and shouting too.

I have never seen a dead person look so pretty. My cousin Jasmine looks like an angel lying in her white casket. The pink lace lining matches her pink, green, and white dress. She called that dress her AKA sorority outfit. Jasmine bought the dress on sale at Macy's in Crabtree Valley Mall over in Raleigh, and she was saving it to wear to the end-of-the-summer dance on North Carolina Central University's campus, two weeks from now. My cousin was treating herself after making all As her senior year in college. She was so excited about starting graduate school at NCCU in the fall. I was excited for her. We all were.

Poor Jasmine had no idea she was buying a dress for her own funeral. She had no idea she wouldn't live long enough to go to the dance or attend graduate school in the fall or anything else. I had no idea my cousin would die so young.

Jasmine was just doing what she did best. She was planning ahead. Jasmine always wanted to be ready for the next exciting thing that was going to happen in her life. Even the end-of-the-summer school dance was exciting to my cousin. She wasn't the kind of girl who would run to the mall at the last minute to buy something to wear. I would tease her and tell her that some of the clothes she bought so early would be out of style by the time she wore them. But she didn't care what I said. She just always had to be prepared. Everything had to match. The shoes, the bag, everything. Even her sunglasses. That was my cousin all right! Always ready, down to her outfit and what time she would arrive. Never late for anything.

Jasmine enjoyed life and she enjoyed her family.

She enjoyed her friends and school. And now she's gone. At twenty years old, she is gone.

Gone forever.

I loved hanging out with Jasmine's college friends—the "honeys," as my friends at school call them. Life at North Carolina Central seemed like so much fun for them. I just wanted to be around the college kids as much as possible. I wanted to be a part of their lives. I spent all summer trying to hang out with them, and I definitely want to go to Central when I graduate from high school in three years. Going to NCCU is a family tradition. My grandpa and grandma were graduates from Central, and so were Aunt Shirley and Momma.

Jasmine made college look easy. She was the reason I was looking forward to college. She was just a happy person. Even when I wanted to cry, Jasmine would say something silly and make me laugh.

It was really hard to laugh when I came to live with Jasmine and my aunt and uncle, because nothing's easy when you're trying to deal with my drug-addicted momma. Daddy left to go back to Iraq at the end of my freshman year two months ago. He pretty much ordered me to live with Aunt Shirley and Uncle Todd until he came back from the war. I had every intention of doing just that until my friends started telling me they'd seen Momma hanging out on the street corners again with really bad people. To make matters worse, she was doing drugs and living with that no-good boyfriend, Bow.

After living in a homeless shelter last year and finally moving in with my cousin, I thought we were going to be safe. Momma had barely escaped going to jail after she fell asleep and burned down the homeless shelter. That's how we ended up at my aunt's house. But Momma went back into the hood to live with Bow, and I moved back too, because I thought that was the only way to help her. Daddy was having none of that and he was back in the States before I knew it. He hauled me back to my aunt Shirley and uncle Todd's house. I don't know if that was good or bad, because if I had stayed there with Momma, maybe I could have saved Jasmine from crazy Bow.

It's hard to believe that Jasmine's dead. It's hard to believe that I'll never be able to talk to her again. We talked all the time about everything. If I went back to Momma's for a few weeks, Jasmine would find a way to call me, even if my cell phone was turned off, which was usually the case. Most people thought that we were sister and brother, not first cousins. Not two sisters' children—sisters who have been paralyzed by pain all week.

I can't imagine how they feel. I just know that I'm hurting so bad. I feel like this is my fault. I wonder if Momma feels any guilt about how Jasmine died.

My moving back in with Aunt Shirley and Uncle Todd brought all of my troubles with me. I brought all of Momma's troubles to their house too. Problems I have been dealing with as a son of a drugged-out mother. The problems that I guess other teenagers have too when their daddy's away fighting a senseless war.

I miss my daddy and I'll be glad when he comes home. When he returns from Iraq this time he won't have to go back. I'm counting the days from when he left two months ago and told me he'd be home for good in six months. I'm so excited knowing he's coming home forever. Maybe he can fix some of the madness in our lives. I wonder where we'll live. Maybe we'll move in with his girlfriend, Pauline, or stay here with my folks.

Yes, I brought all of that mess into my aunt and

uncle's home, and now their baby is dead—dead from a bullet to the head.

The bullet came from Momma's Bow's gun. Bow's no good, and when he's caught he'll go to jail where he belongs. I just don't believe God will leave things like this.

I know that Bow pulled the trigger, but I feel responsible for Jasmine's death. I feel like Momma killed her too. Maybe we both killed her with our problems.

I still wake up in the middle of the night thinking about how she died. I don't know how to explain it. There's a feeling of loneliness without Jasmine. A feeling that I'm the only person left on earth. My chest hurts. My heart hurts. I just hurt all over. I don't know how we got here as a family.

READING GROUP GUIDE

PRE-READING
ACTIVITIES & RESEARCH

1. Joseph Flood's mother is a drug and alcohol addict, and her addictions cause her to act in desperate and dangerous ways. Using an encyclopedia or a medical resource, research cocaine and alcohol. Specifically, what does each substance do to the human body, including the brain? What happens when people become addicted? Why are certain people susceptible to addiction? What are the warning signs? How do people overcome addictions?

2. Research homeless youths in America: How many are there? How do children and teenagers become homeless? Do they have certain factors in common, such as that they are members of a

single-parent family or that one of their parents is addicted to drugs or alcohol or is mentally ill? Are there large numbers of homeless people in your area? What organizations or charities exist to help them?

DISCUSSION TOPICS

1. Joseph Flood tells his own story in *Joseph*; in novel writing, this is called a first-person narrative. Would the book have been different if another character told Joseph's story? Do you prefer hearing a main character express his or her views directly, or do you like when a third-person narrator describes them?

2. Joseph's mother's serious drug problem has forced her to enter a rehabilitation center many times. Do you know anyone who has been through rehab? What do you think happens there? Why do

you think some people become addicted to drugs or alcohol?

3. "I hate it when she calls me dude; like we are friends, instead of mother and son." Do you think that parents should speak from a place of authority when they interact with their children? Do your parents talk to you as if you are a friend? Do they use slang or try to speak as if they are younger than they really are? How does that make you feel?

4. There are many instances in the book where people judge others based on things like clothing, skin color, or social status. Give some examples. Can you really know a person if you focus only on the surface things about them? Has anyone made assumptions about you without ever talking to you? How did that make you feel?

5. "'Do not wait on the mountain to come to

you—climb the mountain yourself.' Grandaddy said that every day of his life." What does this expression mean? How does Joseph follow his grandfather's advice?

6. "I want to tell Principal Scott that I fight all day, every day to survive. I fight to eat. I fight to have a place to sleep. I fight for heat. I fight for my life. But I say nothing as he dismisses me for class." Why doesn't Joseph tell Principal Scott what is happening to him? Why doesn't he want the adults to know how difficult things are in his personal life? If you were Joseph, would you seek out an adult to share your problems?

7. Joseph says of his cousin, Jasmine, who lives with both her parents in a nice suburban house, "I just want a normal life like [her]." Have you ever wanted to live someone else's life? Why? If you could switch lives with someone, with whom would you

trade, and why would you choose this person? Do you think you'd be happier?

8. After Joseph's father is deployed to Iraq, he and Joseph communicate mainly through letters and e-mails. Do you like to write letters or e-mails, or do you prefer to talk to people? How do you feel when you get mail?

9. What is the definition of "family" to Joseph? Do you think that it means living with both a mother and father? Who makes up Joseph's family? Does a family have to include two parents?

10. Many of the adults who know Joseph try to shield him from the true feelings they have about his mother. Is that a good thing for them to do? Would it be better for Joseph if people like his Aunt Shirley were more straightforward about what a bad influence his momma was, and how Joseph would be better off not living with her?

11. After Nick finds out that Joseph's father is in Iraq, he says, "I think everybody in this school knows at least one person in Iraq." Do you know anyone serving in the U.S. armed forces, whether they're stationed in Iraq or elsewhere? How does that make you and the person's loved ones feel, knowing this person is in a faraway place doing a dangerous job?

12. Would the story change if Joseph's father had the drug problem instead of his mother? Do you think Joseph's life would turn out differently?

13. Talk about the many ways Momma betrays Joseph's trust. In spite of all the terrible things she does, why does Joseph want to help her so badly?

14. What did you think of Momma? Did you have any sympathy for her at all? When Joseph overhears her admit that she never wanted to give birth to him, what did you think of Joseph's reaction? How

did that disclosure make you feel about Joseph and about Momma?

15. How would you react if you found out one of your friends was keeping a deep secret about their home life, much like Joseph did? Would there be anything that would prevent you from helping your friend?

ACTIVITIES & PROJECTS

1. Write a play, or a short story, where you are a parent and your mother or father is the child. Reverse roles between other figures in your story—a student becomes a teacher, a doctor becomes a patient, etc.

2. Create posters to hang up at your school or place advertisements in your school or local newspaper that promote awareness of teen homelessness or drug/alcohol addiction. Include hotlines or

information about support groups in your area that help people experiencing either problem.

3. Organize a clothing drive in your school, where students can donate old or outgrown clothes that children and teenagers in homeless shelters could wear, like Joseph did while he stayed at the shelter with his mother.

4. Write a short story where the main characters communicate with each other only through letters or e-mails, and don't speak to each other directly.

5. There are many online organizations that allow people to write cards and letters or send care packages to American troops stationed overseas. Research some of these groups and organize a letter-writing campaign or care-package drive in your school.

HAVE YOU READ THESE
GREAT BOOKS?

SUZANNE MORGAN **WILLIAMS**

KIRKPATRICK **HILL**

P.B. **KERR**

SHELIA P. **MOSES**

MARGARET K. McELDERRY BOOKS
PUBLISHED BY SIMON & SCHUSTER

CHECK OUT THESE ADRENALINE-CHARGED NOVELS FROM ATHENEUM!

ATHENEUM BOOKS FOR YOUNG READERS
Published by SIMON & SCHUSTER

DARK DUDE
Oscar Hijuelos

SHOOTING STAR
Fredrick McKissack Jr.

ICECORE
Matt Whyman

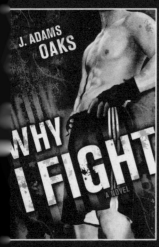

WHY I FIGHT

SHIFT

GENESIS ALPHA

Gripping fiction by NEW YORK TIMES bestselling author

SHARON M. DRAPER

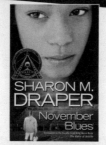

THE BATTLE OF JERICHO
Coretta Scott King Honor Book

NOVEMBER BLUES
Coretta Scott King Honor Book

JUST ANOTHER HERO

OUT OF MY MIND

COPPER SUN
Coretta Scott King Award Winner
NAACP Image Award Nominee

ROMIETTE & JULIO

FORGED BY FIRE
Coretta Scott King Award Winner

TEARS OF A TIGER
John Steptoe Author Award
for New Talent

DARKNESS BEFORE DAWN

From Atheneum Books for Young Readers • Published by Simon & Schuster

Did you love this book?

Want to get access to the hottest books for free?

Log on to simonandschuster.com/pulseit

to find out how to join,

get access to cool sweepstakes,

and hear about your favorite authors!

Become part of Pulse IT and tell us what you think!

Margaret K.
McElderry Books   SIMON & SCHUSTER BFYR SIMON PULSE